SAN FRANCISCO WRITERS CONFERENCE

SFWriters.org

2023 Writing Contest Anthology

What We've Believed

First Edition

Designed and Produced by E. A. Provost at
New Alexandria Creative Group
For the San Francisco Writers Foundation
©Copyright 2023 by the San Francisco Writers Foundation
All rights reserved by the individual authors.
www.NewAlexandriaCG.com
www.SFWriters.org
Available everywhere via print on demand.
Please support your local bookstores.
ISBN: 978-1-64715-009-9

Dear Reader,

A sense of theme always emerges as we assemble these anthologies for the writing contest. The shifts fascinate us as we imagine what might cause them. We don't assign a theme. In that sense, this contest is more open than many, and we get submissions from all over the world, from writers of every age at every stage of their career, on many topics in various subgenres. We wondered if the theme this year, of belief, might be too broad or might imply a religious trend, which is not the case.

There are so many books about beliefs. So many statements of belief. Heaps of content with a rigid, take-a-stand directive attached to it. This is not that. This is self-examination, cultural examination, and coming to terms with a worldview that we know is limited and will change as we grow. This is about beauty, wonder, justice, and grief, all things tied to our beliefs about the family, community, nation, planet, and universe we happened to be born in.

This is the primary reason we read. To explore new worlds, whether that's a hospital, like in our Grand Prize-winning nonfiction piece *Seasons,* a mass confessional at a atholic convention like the nonfiction category winner *Confessin' Ain't Easy,* on the edge of a cliff like our adult fiction category winner, *Young Men,* on a *Tumultuous Trail,* like our poetry category winner, or in a writer's imaginary world like *Veilweaver,* the children's/young adult category winner. Every finalist took us somewhere interesting, giving us insight into their beliefs and the things that shape them. We could go on and on about it, but you should read them yourself.

Fortunately, all of them are printed here in our third contest anthology celebrating our 18th annual contest. Entries were limited to the first 1500 words of an unpublished or self-published manuscript or up to 3 poems (judged individually) with a collective word count within that. That's a generous chance to make a good first impression on an agent or editor, so this anthology is also an opportunity for aspiring writers to see what caught our agent judges.

CONGRATULATIONS! To each of the entrants published here, especially our Grand Prize and Category Winners. We hope this book will entice readers to seek out the work of our finalists as they achieve greater success in the coming years. Several previous finalists have already informed us that they've signed publishing deals or chosen to self-publish, and we can't wait to read their and your completed works.

THANK YOU! To every writer who submitted work, we cannot hold a writing contest without broad participation, and again, better-quality entries were submitted this year than ever. Your persistence as you continue to improve and submit is the critical factor in achieving success as an author, and we honor your efforts. To our volunteers and judges who made this contest happen. To New Alexandria Creative Group, who partnered with us to publish this beautiful anthology. The generosity of our community fills our hearts.

Sincerely,

The San Francisco Writers Conference Executive Board

Find out more about the San Francisco Writers Conference and our year-round events, including the next writing contest, at SFWriters.org.

TABLE OF CONTENTS

Adult
Nonfiction

Grand Prize Winner:
Seasons

By Terry Ratner

There are two main seasons in Phoenix: summer and winter. Our fall and spring are bypassed for long stretches of sameness. Maybe there's a hint of spring in March, when a frail rain falls, casting a silver net over the neighborhood. Then the sky clears and the flowers smell like baby lotion until the aroma is suffocated in blazing heat. These are our seasons.

Nursing also has its own seasons. They follow no direct weather pattern and occur as suddenly as a hurricane or an earthquake, without much warning. There are brief periods of calm with little activity, just the daily comings and goings of patients—the ones who recover without much pain, without any scars.

Then the changes occur: trees with still branches begin their dance; the full moon wears an orange veil as winds throw blankets of dust like confetti up toward the sky. In daylight the air fades to sepia, like an old photograph. That's when code bells chime and intensive care units fill to capacity with dying patients and grieving families. The scent of loss is everywhere, and one can't escape the inevitable season of death.

It begins in the arteries, rushing words without words. Some agree: "It's too soon for death." Others welcome the freedom from pain. I want to climb into bed with patients and hold them. In preop, before they lose their legs or breasts, or after, tell them they are still whole.

The season of loss passes like a series of cold breaths, one after another.

The way I practice nursing might have been different if I hadn't lost my mother in the spring of 1993. The time of year when the nights stay cool and days begin to warm. That's when I began to bond with little old ladies wearing turquoise rings, silver earrings, and glittering beads. I'd hold their hands and laugh with them like old friends. I'd study their faces, searching for a connection: hair the color of freshly fallen snow, skin paper-thin, eyes shining like topaz, and a dimple on the left when they smiled.

My nursing care changed again in the spring of 1999 when my son, Sky, died in a motorcycle crash. All the young patients became a part of me—each one taking up a small space in my heart, trying to fill the emptiness. They brought about poems of music, stanzas without metaphor, making something out of nothing.

It all happened during the season that's sometimes missed. During the season that hides; the one that smells like jasmine and sprouts tulips from the darkness of the earth. It's a season that cools the evening sky with its sweet resinous wind while orange tree petals drift to the ground like snow. The season filled with colors: fairy dusters with pink puffs radiating from their centers and clusters of purple wisteria trailing their vines around budding trees. That was the season when my world caved in.

Those deaths affected my career in ways I never understood until now. They left a sickness in my heart that can't be healed from medicine. No drug can take it away. No narcotic is strong enough to dull the pain.

My patients are the medicine I need: Elderly women with blue hair who want to hold my hand and call me "honey" because no one else is there with them. The old men with salt and pepper sprinkled on the few hairs they have left who tell me a joke because their children are too busy to listen. The young people who are having surgery because they were reckless, the ones I caution and catch myself preaching to—these are the patients who fill my void.

I prepared a young man for surgery last week. Behind the paisley curtains, he cursed as he shook his head from side to side and moaned, sounding more like a pop star singing a song of love and loss.

"Help me, someone! I can't take this pain any longer!" he yelled.

I pulled a chair close to his bed, placed a cool wash cloth across his forehead, and injected morphine into his intravenous port. I asked him how the accident happened.

"I was riding my dirt bike out in the desert and got carried away performing some fancy stunts. I fractured my left leg."

I looked at the external fixator attached to his leg, the swelling in his ankle and knee, and the metal pins that disappeared into his bone. I watched his temple pulsating and thought about life, about luck, about my son, and wondered why he had to die.

I took the young man's calloused hand in mine and listened as he talked about the accident.

"I don't know what happened. The bike just got away from me," he said.

The connection between him and Sky went deeper than motorcycles: their bushy eyebrows, big brown eyes and olive complexion, a build referred to as "buff," and flawless skin. I wanted to save this young man and his parents from a worse fate. I wanted his parents to be immune to the disease that afflicted me.

"You're playing Russian roulette with your life," I told him. I felt his hand squeeze mine. His forehead dripped with tiny beads of perspiration.

"My belief is we all die when our time is up. I'm not afraid of death," he said. "We all have to die sometime."

I wanted to put my arms around him and talk about a son who followed that belief. A son who thought he had nine lives and joked about his luck—a son who had two motorcycle crashes before the fatal one. A son who kissed me on the cheek two days before he died, for no particular reason. But I didn't. Instead, I just told him to be careful. I don't want to burden others with my grief.

Twenty-four years have passed since Sky's death, but the sense of loss lingers, like a potpourri scent that never quite goes away. I want to be reminded of him, the joys and the heartbreaks. I want to be around others with his interests, language, gestures that link them as one. And just like a child who grows up and leaves, so do the patients I connect with. They come and they go like the change of seasons—something to count on, like the first rainfall of the year, or the scent of an early bloom leaving us with a bouquet to remember. What remains at the heart of this is its humanity, its search for connections within the seasons of our lives.

Terry Ratner is an American writer, essayist, journalist, editor, and registered nurse who grew up in Chicago. Writing has always served a purpose in her life, but it wasn't until her son died (1999) in a motorcycle accident that she began to publish her work. Recipient of the Southwestern Writer's Award and Soul-Making Literary Competition, she is currently working on *Paper Coffins*, a memoir dealing with issues of family and identity. Find more of her work at terryratner.com.

Category Winner:
Confessing Ain't Easy

By ML Barrs

Maybe it was something about attending Mass three times in as many days. That's a lot of religion for someone who's not used to it. This Mass drew so many worshippers they almost filled the convention hall. The altar was on a dais and there were candles, incense, and priests in brocaded vestments, but the cavernous space was seriously lacking in stained glass and statues of saints. It felt more like an event than a sacrament.

Mom came up the bleacher steps after receiving communion, looking serene in her long flowery dress and light sweater. She knelt down in front of her seat. No padded risers here. It felt wrong to sit while she knelt, so I got on my knees next to her. When we sat back up, she held my hand until the priest said the last blessing and sent us on our way.

Day three of the Catholic Celebration of Family, put on by the Eternal Word Television Network in Birmingham, Alabama. I was about at my fill. After mass, Mom tugged me back toward a crowded room packed with booths filled with icons and prayer cards and books. The faint aroma of incense floated amid the bouquet of sweat, perfume, and the distinctive smell of cigarette smokers.

Maybe I simply didn't want to look at any more rosaries and statues. We'd already spent hours doing that. I stopped and pointed. "I think I'll do that instead." I might have been even more surprised than she was when I headed toward the arrowed sign that said 'confession.'

The line stretched down the hall, so I had plenty of time to question what I was doing, certain that people could tell I didn't belong with them. There were a few young people, but most looked older than my fifty-plus years. Some held rosaries and read missals. I tried to remember the words I'd learned for my First Confession. I only got as far as, "Forgive me, Father, for I have sinned…"

The line moved so slowly I almost jumped out of it a few times, but it would get moving again just then, so I stayed. I made lists in my mind of what I would confess. This wasn't like when I was a kid, and most of my sins had to do with fighting with my brothers or complaining about chores. Now, there was a lot more ground to cover. When I finally turned the corner, I saw people formed two lines to go into two separate rooms. When I was up next, whoever was in that room must have done a lot wrong because three people went in and out of the other room while I waited.

When a woman finally came out a man rushed out right after her. He had on a priest's white collar and black clothes and looked flustered as he said, "Go on in. I'll be right back." It was kind of funny. It must be tough, needing to use the restroom while listening to people beg forgiveness for their misdeeds.

I entered the small meeting room, with a chair set up next to a screen. Good. My knees still hurt from kneeling next to Mom. The priest came back, and I got a good look at him. I'd never before seen a priest who heard my confession. He was a regular-looking guy with curly grayish-brown hair, about my age or a little younger. He went around the screen, opened up the little confessional window, and thanked me for waiting.

I said, "No problem," then added, "I'm not sure whether this is the right time or place because it's been 38 years since my last confession."

He actually chuckled. "Oh, this is definitely the right time and the right place."

Oh, good, he has a sense of humor. "I don't remember the words."

"The words aren't what's important," he said. "What's important is that you're here now. Tell me what's on your mind."

"It's been so long I don't even know where to start."

"That's okay. Do you remember the Ten Commandments?"

"Most of them, I think."

"We can start there." There was a smile in his voice. "I can help if you don't remember them all."

"Ok, I'll just kind of go down the list." I immediately began re-sorting and editing my mental catalog of wrongdoings, discarding some as relatively insignificant, trying to remember if any of the commandments even applied to others. "We can start with the big one. I haven't killed anyone."

Maria Barrs, writing as ML Barrs, is the author of *Parallel Secrets*, featuring a TV journalist who must reveal her own dark secrets to save a kidnapped child. Learn more about Maria's writing and background at her website, mlbarrs.com.

Ninety-Nine Fire Hoops

By Allison Hong Merrill

I discovered that I became a starter wife from a light switch.

Not a light bulb, like I had a big idea. A light switch. A light switch in my apartment that I flipped on and off, but the living room remained dark, and that darkness caused a pricking, tingling sensation in my hands and feet.

When I left the apartment two hours earlier, the lights worked, the heater ran, and Cameron—my husband of sixteen months—was doing homework on our bed. Lately, we kept fighting about investing in the boat his father planned to purchase. I said no, and we had been giving each other the cold shoulder for days. Tired of our never-ending arguments, now I wanted reconciliation. This particular day, around dinnertime, I went to seek marriage advice from my classmate, a fellow Taiwanese student. Before leaving, I stood before Cameron and said goodbye. If he heard me, he acted otherwise. So I wrote *I love you, Cam* on a Post-it note and left it on the inside of the front door. It wasn't there now.

Now, I had to feel my way to the bedroom.

Felt the bed.

Felt one pillow.

Felt a chill.

I didn't need to keep feeling anymore. Didn't need to avoid bumping into the desk, or the chairs, or Cameron's bike. They weren't in the dark with me.

In the dark, there was no warmth.

No gas for the heater.

No electricity.

No telephone.

No food.

My heartbeat quickened and thundered in my ears.

What happened? Am I in the wrong apartment? Must be. All the units look the same on the outside . . .

I felt my way out of the apartment and double-checked the gold number nailed to the door: 21. My apartment, no mistake.

No!—no, no, no, no, no! Where's Cameron?

I tucked my hands under my armpits in the November evening chills. My legs trembled as I paced in a circle in small steps. The windows of other units in the building glowed in golden light. Through my next-door neighbors' blinds, I noticed them sitting around the coffee table, *Seinfeld* playing on TV, the waft of their gumbo dinner in the air. It looked warm and inviting where they were. I stood in the cold, dark night, staring past my door into the abyss. For tonight's dinner, I'd planned to make chicken stir-fry. Cameron would've enjoyed it on the couch right there, over there, there, there, there, where it was nothing but emptiness now.

The black of the apartment reminded me of a summer night, three months earlier when the power had gone out in the entire complex. That night, Cameron drove back to his parents' home in the next town for an air-conditioned room. I didn't go with him because I would've rather eaten dog food than see my in-laws. To say they were bad people would be telling only half the truth. A big part of the problem was me—I avoided them to avoid speaking English.

I was born and raised in Taiwan and was only confident speaking Mandarin Chinese. On this fateful night, I was a fresh-off-the-boat immigrant—having been in the U.S. for only sixteen months—and heavily dependent on Cameron's Chinese-speaking prowess for almost everything. For example, when underwear shopping, he had to tag along to tell the lingerie store clerk I wished to get my size measured in the metric system. America's customary system didn't mean anything to me. Another time, I accidentally cut my finger with a rusty utility knife while opening a package. Cameron had to explain to the emergency room nurse why I needed a tetanus shot. For me, to carry on English conversations wasn't just a linguistic challenge or an intellectual evaluation; it was an insurmountable task.

Of course, avoiding my in-laws couldn't possibly be healthy for my marriage. But there were other contributing factors to my shaky relationship with Cameron, too. To say it was all my doing would be giving me more credit than I deserve. After all, there are always two people in a relationship; one simply can't start a marital war alone. However, I'll say my short marriage to Cameron helped shorten the emotional distance between him and his father.

Glad to have helped!

Upon discovering the non-working light switch, I realized I needed to overcome my dependence on Cameron as my mouthpiece, as well as the fear that crippled my ability to communicate with English speakers, and go immediately to the apartment office in the next building to talk with the manager.

"Hi, I'm Allison." My voice shocked me more than it did the manager, Jane—an overweight woman in her late fifties whose eyes at this moment were as huge as tennis balls. She'd never heard me speak. In fact, she'd probably never really looked at me before. I was always behind Cameron, who did all the talking with his proud Texan accent and charismatic humor. But the real surprise was hearing myself say the name that my tenth-grade English teacher had given me the way Americans do, without mixing up the *L* and *R*—one of the English-language learning curves that most Chinese people struggle with. Not *Ayhreesong*. I said, *Allison*. The parting of my lips + the tip of my tongue kicking off the back of my upper front teeth + the soft dropping of my tongue + short hissing sss juxtaposed with the nasal ending = Allison. I said that.

Jane took off her reading glasses. "Forgot somethin'?"

I shook my head. "Cam—Cameron gone."

"Well, o'course. So should you. Why you still here?"

I knew what she said but didn't understand what she meant. I blurted out "yes" but immediately felt idiotic and frustrated to be stuck with it. "My house, cold." I pointed in the direction of my apartment and hugged myself. I shivered exaggeratedly and chattered my teeth purposely.

Jane shook her head. "K—ma'am, I'm confused. Why you still here anyway? Weren't Cameron's parents here earlier to move you guys out?"

Weren't Cameron's parents here earlier to move you guys out?

Weren't Cameron's parents here earlier to move you guys out?

Weren't Cameron's parents here earlier to move you guys out?

I—got—moved—out?

"Really?" I exclaimed, not caring about mixing up my L and R.

Jane pushed her office chair away with her bottom and walked to a wall cabinet behind her seat. She fished out a key from rows of hooks and waved it in the air. "See? Number 21. Your apartment. Cameron turned in the key." She put her other hand on her hip and leaned forward. "Question, ma'am: Why you still here?"

I was still here, in the apartment manager's office, in Edinburg, in Texas, in the U.S.A., and I was mighty lost.

"Sorry," I said, my scalp starting to feel numb. "Please, one week"—I held up my index finger—"I find help. I want stay—myself."

I hoped she would not only understand but also have mercy on me. My cheeks and earlobes were burning. My throat was tight, as though I were dry-swallowing a pill. And my head was so heavy I could only look down at my shoes. At this point, everything about my life shared the same theme of emptiness: empty apartment, empty pockets, empty hands—palms up—asking for empathy.

Maybe Jane detected an unusual sense of urgency in the abandoned foreigner on her premises; maybe she fathomed the depth of my trouble and grasped the serious reality that, at this moment, she was the only one who could make the situation a little more bearable for me. Whatever it was, she slumped into her chair, clicked her tongue, pushed a pile of papers on her desk from one side to another, stroked her temple, and then, with her seemingly softened heart, said, "Ay—you stay."

Allison Hong Merrill is a loveaholic, a Taiwanese immigrant, and a Wall Street Journal best-selling author. Holding an MFA from Vermont College of Fine Arts, Allison's work appears in *The New York Times* and the *Huffington Post* and has won national and international literary prizes. Her debut memoir, *Ninety-Nine Fire Hoops*, has won over 45 book awards. She is a keynote speaker, instructor, and panelist at various writer's conferences nationwide and in Asia. She also appears on TV, radio, and podcasts; in magazines, newspapers, and journals. Visit her at AllisonHongMerrill.com to sign up for her monthly email.

Bright Eyes: A Memoir

By Bridey Thelen-Heidel

Chapter 1: YES

"Bridey!" My mom cries on the other end of the phone. "Come now! I need you!"

"Mom? What's wrong? Where are you?" Panicking because I haven't seen her since last night, and it's nearly noon, I look out our living room window like she might be calling from the front yard.

"I'm. At. Debbie's." She says, choking on her words.

"I'm coming!" Slamming the phone on the receiver, I drop my Barbie on the carpet; not caring she lands on the oil stains Al's Harley-Davidson left behind when he rode out of our living room for the last time.

Leaping off the front porch, my bare feet land on prickly bits of pine cone. "Ouch! Ouch!" I shout across the dirt driveway, hopscotching as I pull shards from the bottoms of my feet that don't yet have summer calluses because school just got out.

Sprinting around the corner to Debbie's house, I slip by the neighbor's wood fence, where my initials *BT* are carved underneath the initials *BM*. The boy who put them there with his pocket knife pretended he didn't know how to play doctor the first time I showed him. The second time, he carved our initials together.

I push Debbie's door open without knocking and see my mom slumped over the kitchen table—still wearing the burgundy blouse I picked out last night. Crouching down on the gold-speckled linoleum beside her chair, I smooth her bleached-blond hair from her face. "Hey, Mom."

Her pink, puffy eyes stare into mine, maybe trying to remember who I am. "Hey, Bright Eyes." She whispers, letting snot drip onto her onto her jeans.

"Hi," I whisper back, forcing myself to smile. Seeing my mom cry always makes me want to, but I hardly ever do because it's my job to make her happy. "I'm here, Mom. It's okay now."

She takes a big breath and wipes her nose with the back of her hand. Tears fill her eyes, and she shakes her head back and forth. "Oh, no, baby, it's not okay." Pulling me to her chest, she begins sobbing hard. Smothered in her Tabu perfume—which I usually love—the smell reminds me of the last inch of milk in the carton when she leaves it out overnight. It's burning my nose, but I wouldn't ever pull away from her.

Another whisper. "Mom? Did someone die?"

She leans back and searches my face for the answer. Looking over her shoulder to make sure we're alone, she leans in. "I'm pregnant."

"What?" I ask too loud, now searching her face.

She clears her throat to unstick the answer. "It's Al's."

His name punches me in the chest and knocks me on my butt the way he's done to my mom a thousand times. Getting away from both of them, I scoot across the cold linoleum, shoving his name back at her with both hands. "No! No! No!"

Mom reaches for me. "I know, baby. I know. I'm sorry."

My back against the farthest wall in the kitchen, I bury my head between my knees and close my eyes to keep him away from me. *No, no, no, no.* But he's there— black hair, black eyes, black vest, black boots. My whole body is shivering, shaking from the cold tile under my butt—terrified he's coming back. I wrap myself up tighter, tears streaming down my cheeks and onto my bare legs. Swallowing the burn coming up my throat, I whisper—*Don't cry. Don't cry. Don't cry*—because if I start, I'll never stop.

"Come here, baby." Mom calls to me in the soft voice I've used with her since Al moved in a year ago—a year of whispering in the dark for her to come to me. I peek my eyes open and meet hers. She pats her lap. "Come to your mama."

I shake my head, no, but she nods yes. I'm mad at her for doing this to us, but she's all I have. I crawl across the tile and climb into her lap. Wiggling myself into position makes us both giggle because my long, skinny body doesn't fit. I lean against her chest, letting my legs dangle and sweeping my bare toes across the tile. "Mom?"

"What baby?"

"Please don't let him come back."

She lets out all her breath onto the back of my neck and wraps her arms around my chest, sniffling back tears I know won't stop if she starts either.

Staring at Debbie's ceiling, it looks like someone covered it in popcorn painted white. Counting the kernels, I quickly lose the number, like trying to count the freckles on my arms. Al doesn't have any freckles, so I doubt the baby will. We won't match at all.

Goosebumps have covered my freckles. The sun left Debbie's kitchen, and it's getting dark. "Hey, Mom? I'm kinda cold. You wanna go home?"

She wipes her nose on the back of my t-shirt—already soaked in her tears and sticking to my skin—and then begins moaning the way I do when my stomach hurts. Her arms squeeze tighter around me as she rocks us in the heavy wood kitchen chair. Her warm breath on my neck drops my eyelids closed, and I lose myself in the rhythm of the rocking—the two of us bobbing up and over waves that grow bigger as she moans louder. Floating in our imaginary ocean, Mom's hands slip down my sides and grip my t-shirt like she's holding onto a lifejacket instead of wearing one.

I'm saving her from drowning.

Again.

Opening my eyes, it's now nearly dark, but we're still alone. Freezing, I wiggle in Mom's lap to wake her from wherever she drifted off to. She loosens her grip without letting me sit up. "So, do you want to keep this baby?"

I don't understand her question and repeat it to myself. *Keep the baby?* Before I can ask her what *not keeping* a baby means, she slides me off her lap and into the chair next to her. Knee-to-knee, I watch as she gulps a mouthful of air and mittens her hands with her sleeves to dry her eyes and wipe her nose. Her pout bends up into a smile as she says, "I have an idea!"

Copying her, I swallow a mouthful of air and dry my eyes with the bottom of my t-shirt. "What?"

"*You* can be the baby's dad!" Mom says, her eyes wide and excited. She shakes her head and crinkles her nose like she smells something gross. "We don't need Al!" Patting my thighs, she squeezes my knees. "I'll even put your name on the baby's birth certificate!"

"Huh?" I ask, still confused. Like the magic word of the day on *Sesame Street*, everything she's saying is floating in the air around us—moving too quickly to read. I squint, trying to bring her blurry words into focus. "What do you mean *I* can be the dad?"

Mom nods and points to herself. "You know, I'm the mom," she says. Then, she points at me. "And you're the dad! We'll raise the baby on our own—just us!"

Her eyes, still puffy and pink from crying, are begging me to agree with her. I ask, "No Al? Won't he care about the baby?"

Mom holds my hands in hers and leans in until our foreheads touch. "I'm not even gonna tell him I'm pregnant!" She giggles like we're two little girls making secret plans we made with bedsheets.

"What?" I lean back and pull the soaked neck of my t-shirt off my skin.

She sits up straight and smooths her blouse and hair—looking like she's ready to leave Debbie's kitchen—then whispers, "We'll keep the baby a secret from Al."

I nod like I understand because I know she wants me to, but I have another question. "How can I be a dad? I'm not even a boy." Snot slips onto my lip. I smear it across the freckles on the back of my hand. "And I'm only ten."

Mom laughs. "I know you're ten, Bridey, but we can do this!" She stands. "Okay, baby, you ready?"

Still sitting, I stare up at my mom and think about how I've never seen her without a boyfriend. It always feels like she meets a guy and moves him right in. Like, somehow, he makes us a family. I wish she understood that she's all the family I need. My eyes move down her body, stopping at her flat belly that doesn't look at all like she's pregnant. Although I still don't understand how I'm supposed to be a dad, I'm not really allowed to say no—even to little stuff—and I can tell by the way she's looking at me—half smiling and tears in her eyes—there's only one way I can answer her question.

"Yes."

Bridey Thelen-Heidel is an award-winning English teacher whose work with LGBT+ youth is celebrated in *Read This, Save Lives* and California Educator. She recently delivered a TEDx talk about the resilience, optimism, and bravery she developed surviving the abusive upbringing that is also the focus of her memoir, *Bright Eyes*, set for release in August 2024 by SheWrites Press. Hoping to encourage others to share their stories, Bridey speaks candidly about domestic violence and child abuse, and she performed an original piece in an off-Broadway production of *Listen to Your Mother NYC*.

Wrestling with the Uranium Spirits - a Cautionary Tale of Nuclear Waste Cleanup on Native American Lands

By Cindy Foster

Chapter One

"The Queen of the Hat"

"They say you unleashed evil," Doris Valle lowered her voice as she leaned across the table so the tourist hovering near the turquoise earring display couldn't hear. "They say it is worse than if you had never touched the pile. At least before there was grass growing over all that uranium so that the spirits could sleep beneath the earth where they belong. Now you people tore the top off, the spirits have been let out, and they are everywhere."

She glanced quickly at the tourist, then leaned in even closer across the table to me, "And, they say it is making people sick."

We had been sitting in the storeroom behind the grocery, drinking cokes and gossiping at a card table situated next to a vault full of pawned jewelry, pottery, and Navajo rugs while being interrupted every five minutes by first one worker then another - was she willing to extend a little trade here? Did she want to order anything from the salesman just in from Salt Lake City?

I loved it there. Even the interruptions held an air of mystery.

A slim, lightning stroke of a woman, Doris owned Valle's Trading Post, located two miles north of the Navajo reservation border, providing ice for rafters running the San Juan River and cold beer to locals in Mexican Hat, Utah, a town so tiny that her congressman's staff couldn't always find on a map. Her trading post was a tiny salute to free enterprise, sporting signs announcing trailers and trailer spaces for rent, showers for river runners and hikers, and a laundry that could be used for a price and, if you were a local, she would extend credit for up to a year in exchange for jewelry, rugs, and other handicrafts.

A tourist entered the narrow hallway full of crafts next to the soft drink case, and Doris walked over to take one of the necklaces out of the display case, then stood and watched as the man moved on and began to finger what was locally regarded as one of the better collections of Navajo rugs in that area of the reservation that borders the San Juan River. Tony Hillerman country. A place of desolate roads and red rock and families where English was still a distant second language.

Government contractors get used to epitaphs, slurs, and reprimands of long-past grievances. If I had been hearing complaints that we were all-knowing and all evil, I could have handled it without so much as the blinking of an eye. But the idea that we were clueless wonders who had somehow upset the spirit world and let evil escape from some sort of cosmic jail cell was a new one.

Doris came back, sat down, and we picked up the conversation.

"But the uranium pile is fenced off, and we monitor air. There isn't any radioactivity leaving that site," I said.

"It doesn't matter; they blame everything on it," she said. "If someone sneezes in Kayenta (45 miles to the south), they say it is the spirits. I had an old couple in the other night, and I noticed they weren't driving their truck.

"When I asked them what happened, they went into a long explanation that the spirits from the tailings had gotten into the truck's steering column. The old man said he could handle the spirits even though they made the truck difficult to drive, but they had lent it to their teenaged grandson, and he was too young to stand up to the spirits -- the truck had gone into a ditch."

I'd spent the morning listening to a group of local men and women ask questions that I couldn't answer about how the radiation might be harming them and their livestock. It seemed as if an equal number of people were furious that they would no longer be in close proximity to a mile-long hill of uranium tailings since the construction project had been put on hold and 140 men and women had lost their jobs. They were ready to sleep in the parking lot if they could just get a cleanup job back.

This was rough country, and people got physical when they were angry. The site's construction project manager had admitted he was worried about people tearing up equipment and buildings. "I even thought about getting a medicine man to bless the site," he had gulped out guiltily, his chin dipping down and those blue eyes averting my gaze as the sentence came out. He had looked as shameful as if he had been confessing drinking on the job. "Hmm, I wonder if we could pay for that," I'd said. "Let me see what I can find out..."

A toss-away comment if ever there was one. Certainly, no one back in Albuquerque would have thought of it. No one ever advanced their career with the U.S. Department of Energy by "giving in to those freeloading Indians" out on the reservation. In fact, "Don't let Jack stick you with just the Indian sites," had been my predecessor's first piece of advice when I began work as a public affairs liaison at Jacobs Engineering, one of the cleanup's prime contractors. "Get stuck with the Indian sites, and you'll sink without a trace," she had said. "Make him give you some of the important ones too."

Now, not only was Doris agreeing with the idea of hiring a medicine man, I was being told that there were spirits - ones that knew right from wrong - and it was all our fault that they were wandering US 160 in search of autos and trucks in which to make mischief.

Finally, I sighed and told her that Tim was expecting me back at the construction trailer, then made my way through the piles of hand-woven blankets and displays of turquoise squash blossom necklaces and dangling silver earrings. I walked out of the building and into the bright light of the late summer Utah sun. I wasn't worried about spirits finding their way into the steering column of the Ford rental car as I opened the door and adjusted the rearview mirror, but I was thinking of the faces of the men and women who lived near the tailings.

I'd half been hoping Doris would laugh at Tim's idea of hiring a medicine man, but she hadn't. Maybe Tim was right, I thought as I drove south of town to where the construction trailers were located. Maybe the only way to get everyone calmed down was to hire a medicine man. Nothing else we had come up with seemed to be working.

I had been told traditional Navajo has no words for things that are unseen, that, like radioactivity, are invisible, but they understand the spirit world as well as any Old Testament archangel. Mother Earth, rocks, mountains, water, everything has a spirit living within it, spirits that must be honored if balance within the universe is to be maintained.

Uranium, the old people will tell you, always had its home on the Navajo reservation and the Navajo and the rock lived together in peace and harmony through the ages, from the time when First Man and First Woman emerged from the underworld and coyote spread the stars for all "the Dine," the chosen people, to see. The rock spirits lived peacefully with people in this arid, vast country until the ore's home was disturbed in the 1950s and 60s as companies arrived to mine and process uranium needed to build the U.S. Government's first nuclear warheads. A decade later, those companies pulled out, leaving behind a legacy of lung cancer, fear, and mistrust, as well as millions of tons of radioactive sand - the dregs that remained after separating ton after ton of ore from its host rock. Some 2,000 former miners have died or are dying now from lung cancer.

I didn't know that day, as I shook off the shivers from the blasts of frigid air conditioning and drove away in my rental car, how many spirits one might wrestle with, some small, some big guys, some with alien faces that we would never be able to identify, others who would look just like our mothers or fathers, friends or ourselves.

I didn't understand how one could start out so innocently to do one small thing and then become caught up in lies and fear; had no idea how hard it can be to find a way through a hostile landscape, never really sure if you are helping or hurting but knowing only that there is no way to retrace your steps, no way to go back to a moment when an idle offer of help could be withdrawn, or giggled away or conveniently forgotten.

Cindy Foster is a New Mexico literary journalist with 30 years of experience as a writer, editor, and reporter. You can find her on LinkedIn.

Kate

By Julie Dearborn

Kate and I spent every Fourth of July together as children. We lit fireworks with the cousins in her enormous backyard, ate hot dogs cooked by the moms, waved sparklers in the air at dusk, and gazed in wonder at the Roman Candles the dads lit and sent soaring into the night sky. Her father, My Uncle Mike, was a history teacher, and he liked to preface the lighting of the Roman Candles with mini-history lessons.

He said things like, "Thomas Jefferson and John Adams both died on July 4, 1826." Or, "Do you know who said 'Give me Liberty or Give me Death? Patrick Henry."

It was always a relief to be with Dad's family. He was much nicer around them. He and Aunt Margaret, Kate's mom, had been close growing up. Margaret, the oldest child, and Dad, the oldest son, buffered the other three siblings from the harshness of a childhood with a largely absent, intermittently abusive alcoholic father and a mother who could never quite make ends meet. But as adults, they only saw each other at holidays, weddings, or funerals. Dad thought Margaret had become a snob. Her children went to the expensive private school where Uncle Mike taught, and they left Wyandotte County, a blue-collar county in Kansas with lots of Eastern European immigrants and African Americans, to live in the more upscale Johnson County, a place full of rather stuck-up white people.

"Margaret and Joe think we're the poor relations," Mom often said.

But we were no more poor than they were rich. We were both in the middle, which at that time, was an expansive and hopeful place to be. The adults I grew up with were much more alike than they were different. They were all Catholic and went to Mass every Sunday, they were all Democrats, and they all remembered precisely where they were when they heard President Kennedy had been shot. The men had all fought in WWII or Korea. The women all wanted their daughters to have the education they'd been denied. Neither Mom nor Aunt Margaret went to college, but there was never any doubt that their daughters would, one way or another.

Kate was kind and funny and probably my smartest cousin. She always got straight As, but she didn't brag about them. It was Mom who always told me about her grades in an attempt to motivate me to improve my lackluster report cards.

By the time we were ready for college, we'd drifted apart. She went off to Sarah Laurence, while I went to the local Junior College before transferring to the University of Kansas. Aunt Margaret really got under my parents' skin during the college application period, with lots of pontificating about how crucial it was to go to the right school. Your entire future depended on it! Kansas City Kansas Junior College was definitely not on her list.

Any gloating Aunt Margaret did was short-lived. Kate didn't even last a semester at Sarah Laurence. She had a breakdown that marked the onset of schizophrenia and took several years off from school before joining me at the University of Kansas. I was a senior, and she was still a freshman. Going away to college was the best thing that had ever happened to me. I didn't have to hide from Dad and his temper. I didn't have to listen to my parents non-stop fighting. My life was moving forward. When Kate called and suggested we get together, I invited her to go to a museum with me and some of my college friends. She came ready to re-connect. She was vulnerable and open, and I was subtly distant; my focus was on my friends. She was my past, and I wanted nothing to do with it.

I can still see her standing in the lobby of the museum, wearing a beige windbreaker, her fine light brown hair tucked behind her ears, her green eyes looking into mine. That was the only time I saw her at KU. I'm not sure how long she stayed, but I know she didn't graduate.

The last time I talked to her was on the phone a few years later.

I was living in San Francisco by then, and Mom had called me during a family party so I could talk to the cousins. Most of them were married and pregnant. Neither Kate nor I were on this path.

"God, they're breeding like rabbits back there," I said when she came to the phone. She laughed really hard, and for a moment, it was as if nothing fundamental had changed.

Today she lives in government subsidized housing in a small town in Kansas. If she stays on her medication, she's stable. She's never had a job or a boyfriend. I heard from her sister that she supports Donald Trump. The Kate I knew is gone. Just like the expansive and hopeful middle where we both grew up.

Julie Dearborn is an English teacher and writer. She lives in San Francisco and has an MFA from Queens University of Charlotte. Her work has been published in *Narrative Magazine, Summerset Review,* and *The Party Train: An Anthology of North American Prose Poetry.* You can find her on LinkedIn.

My Mother's Bridge

By ML Barrs

Four young girls, the youngest perhaps eleven, the oldest still a teen, fell sobbing at the sight of the twisted, fallen steel. They had walked for days, hungry, scared, hiding in trees as soldiers searched below. The railroad bridge, the only route across the river, hung creaking, its once strong straight lines now contorted into a sagging, misshapen V over the water far below. They could go no further.

Her memory that of a child grown old, Mom told the story of the bridge many times in her later years. It might have been months, or maybe years after the start of the war, that she and her sisters faced the bombed-out skeleton of the bridge.

Mom was just ten when the Japanese attacked Pearl Harbor in December 1941. Hours later, they invaded the Philippines. Days later, they took over the city of her birth, Manila, where her family had lived and prospered for generations. Every aspect of her young life was torn apart except for the love of her family and her faith.

As the war went on, Mom's family had to separate, to keep moving to avoid the fighting, to find shelter, to find food. She and her sisters were sent to stay with relatives in another province and had to cross that bridge.

I remember Mom telling that story when I was a child. Mom used to say they prayed and prayed to God for help and somehow made it across. I imagined how terrifying it must have been, clinging to jagged, broken metal, trying not to look down as the remains of the railway bridge swayed and creaked and threatened to give way under the weight of their four small bodies.

Growing up, I assumed that was why she was so afraid of heights, a fear I shared without having had anything remotely like her frightening experience.

After the war, Mom met the American soldier she loved for the rest of her life. Dad, the teenage son of a coal miner, joined the U.S. Army Air Corps and was sent halfway around the world to a place as unlike Logan County, West Virginia, as one can find. They went on to have thirteen children. I am the oldest girl, with three brothers before me, a position I often described as the worst possible but one I wouldn't change for anything, even if I could.

I left my family when I was fifteen and did not see my mother again until my father's funeral five years later. Dad died rescuing my four sisters from drowning in a swollen Oklahoma creek. It is one of the greatest sorrows of my life that he and I never reconciled, that we never spoke as one adult to another, never hugged and said I love you.

The decades that followed were years of joy and heartbreak, of babies and new places, new opportunities, of irrevocable misunderstandings and terrible loss, of grief and healing and growth and new understanding. My Mom and I grew close. We talked and cried and laughed, traveled together, and shared meals and family and love.

That is one of the greatest joys of my life.

In recent years, when she talked about the bridge, Mom would simply say that it was a miracle, that they prayed and prayed, and the angels must have carried them across, that she had no memory of the physical crossing.

On a few occasions when I was called upon to make a speech, I told the story of my mom and her bridge as a metaphor for perseverance and strength and accomplishing goals. In my journalistic compulsion for factual storytelling, I would gloss over the part about the angels and miracles, substituting that with the far more mundane statement that somehow those four young girls managed to make it across.

My mom died too soon, at the age of eighty-six. I thought we still had many years of sitting in kitchens, of sharing family updates and gossip, of remembering and laughing, of just being together.

But Mom got the flu, and the angels carried her across the bridge to join Dad and my brother and sister, who awaited her. She is deeply missed by those of us still on this side.

Maria Barrs, writing as ML Barrs, is the author of *Parallel Secrets*, featuring a TV journalist who must reveal her own dark secrets to save a kidnapped child. Learn more about Maria's writing and background at her website, mlbarrs.com.

Becoming Mrs. Smith

By Robyn Ferrell

On the Nullarbor in those days, the road was unsealed, which meant dusty, throwing a huge plume behind the car. We were always setting out in December; it was very hot by day but cold at night in the tent.

I was curling on the back seat next to the bassinet or leaning over the front seats to be involved in my mother's knitting and my father's driving and my parents' singing – highlights from *The Gondoliers*, key arias from (Soprano and Tenor) the *Messiah*, Edward German's 'Barcarolle' (later in 3 parts when we were three sisters by then) – getting ahead of myself … well, I always was.

This year, not yet able to play with the baby or even talk to her (much less sing), and before seatbelts, I was kneeling up on the backseat. I was looking out of the back window and leaning on the shelf to talk to Mrs Smith.

Mrs Smith was my imaginary friend. Not Binkie or Ranger, but Mrs Smith, no less staid and sensible for being imaginary. She had the strange property of being invisible and inaudible, except to me, and so I was forced to keep up a running commentary on the back seat, relaying her pearls of wisdom for my parents when I wasn't singing her a song; and –

'Mrs Smith says when are we going to get there?'

'Mrs Smith says she'd like a toffee' (out of the blue tin with deers on it)

Mrs Smith says, Mrs Smith says, Mrs Smith … no doubt my parents were tiring of her tendentious comments, or probably the din from the gravel road was shaking every inch as Dad drove at fifty miles an hour over its corrugations, and the windows were wound down to keep up the climate control and were thumping, and so no one heard Mrs Smith say: 'The pram's fallen off the car'.

They didn't hear, they didn't listen to her, a tribulation I have come to realise she suffered often in later life. It was only when they reached Ceduna and pulled into the first sight of civilisation (a caravan park with an ablution block and fish and chip shop with blue, red, green, and yellow strips hanging in the doorway to keep out the flies) that my parents made the discovery for themselves. The pram, which was usually lashed to the spare wheel, was indeed missing, and Mrs Smith had been reporting accurately when she said the pram had fallen off the car.

She must have seen the pram make its reluctant strike for freedom, or perhaps spring desperately from its perch – or perhaps a lingering longing slipping from its moorings – until clunk, it fell onto the road and was left behind, potentially visible in its forlorn white frilled-ness from the rear-vision mirror had anyone cared to look. Parked forsaken, shocked at the change in circumstances in a pothole in the middle of a gravel road in the middle of the Nullarbor, which is about the middle of the Australian continent from coast to coast and miles from anywhere.

Mrs Smith *said* the pram's fallen off the car. And Mrs Smith was a woman of her word.

My parents often laugh about this story and may tell it whenever the topics of 'family trips' or 'imaginary friends' are mentioned, and it remains perennially funny to the little audience who know it by heart but like to hear it repeated.

Mrs Smith was an imaginary friend, but like others in my childhood, as we got older, we lost touch.

At one point during the events I called my career, I had another sighting of Mrs Smith across a seminar room when the paper being given was on Winnicott's psychoanalysis of early childhood. It was mentioned in passing that he viewed imaginary friends as alter egos of a powerful unconscious kind that could presage the development of psychological problems in later life and even the seeds of psychosis.

I was naturally shocked because Mrs Smith, although a comic figure, was never presented as menacing. Indeed, I had inherited the view from my family (originally had from A.A.Milne) that an imaginary friend was a badge of distinction, showing a child's intellectual precocity. I couldn't accept that anyone as respectable and matronly as Mrs Smith – whose only crime had been to witness a pram falling off a car and perhaps to ask for a few too many toffees – was psychotic or even more than mildly daft.

I was rather affronted on her behalf. She seemed to me then, obscured by the gloom of childhood, to be associated only with ordinary homely things like cups of tea and knitting needles and sewing 'skirtles' (another hilarious misconception shared with my sisters that was later cherished in family lore). However she may have been maligned by this (or not), I knew her then only as a creature of the past.

Imagine my alarm, when fifty years later, I met her again.

I set up the dressmaker's dummy in a corner of the bedroom; it had been ordered in a larger size to accommodate my creeping middle age, and I had been momentarily daunted when I pulled it out of the box to see such a substantial model of myself sitting there.

But at five am, in the half-light of an incipient dawn, the figure took form as Mrs Smith. She sidled into the room, an older portly lady standing by my bed, as if with a message for me. 'Hallo, dear.' A lumpish, frumpish, unglamorous woman, unlovely and frankly fat. It was then I realised with incredulous certainty that I was becoming Mrs Smith.

Meeting her again in these uncanny circumstances was a rude awakening. Whatever companionship I had felt with her at four years old had become more complicated in the intervening time. The things she did – the silly way that older ladies run, the depressive recommendation to keep busy, the over-loud personal comments about people queuing in front of her – felt differently when felt from the inside.

And under the pressure of the postmodern, Mrs Smith had started to do things I would never have suspected of her. She was prepared to steal groceries from the supermarket if forced to use the self-checkout machines that she said had been installed just to put ordinary people out of work. She was even known to walk off with shopping baskets, but only if they were the sort with wheels and only because they wouldn't allow you to take the larger trolleys onto the street.

What she said was, when challenged about these habits: 'No one notices an old lady, dear' and sometimes, in an undiluted admission of self-pity: 'Well, I didn't have enough money for the bill.' I felt uneasy about this new dishonesty, but I could see it was her version of rough justice.

She didn't put it this way, but I gather she performed these actions in the service of a left-leaning Luddite rage at the increasing surveillance and net of manipulation thrown over us all by the military-industrial complex. She met mass surveillance with guerrilla action, and market manipulation with targeted illegality.

It was hard on her, the modern world. I saw it took an emotional toll. After her covert struggles with the capitalist forces of manipulation, she needed a Bex and a good lie down (except Bex was no longer on the market, so I fear she substituted alcohol).

In this new iteration, this was Mrs Smith becoming an urban guerilla/special ops agent. This was Mrs Smith 'speaking truth to power.' I never imagined Mrs Smith had any idea of revolution. But on the other hand, who knew anything of her early life? No one showed the least curiosity. She could have been in the Red Emmas. Maybe she threw cobblestones in fury on the streets of Paris in May '68.

All the older nondescript ladies, seen at bus stops and in Woolworths, getting on buses and poring over prices per kilo, were young ladies once. Who knew which of them had supped with Simone de Beauvoir at the Café Deux Magots? Who had led the socialist mob down the main street to the swirl of tear gas? Who had fallen ecstatically into the arms of the maddest, baddest rebel that spoke that day of liberation … ?

Robyn Ferrell is a writer and researcher, author of several books of philosophy, a novel, and a book of creative nonfiction, *The Real Desire*, which was shortlisted for a literary award. She is currently an honorary professor at Sydney University and lives on a cliff opposite the sea. You can find all her books on her author page at amazon.com/author/robynferrell. This excerpt is the opening chapter of a longer book of creative nonfiction, also called *Becoming Mrs Smith*. Robyn welcomes inquiries regarding representation or publication of this work to robynferrell20@gmail.com.

If You Would Only Listen to Me:
A Medical Memoir of Gaslighting, Grit, and Grace

By Rosie Sorenson, MA, MFT

Introduction

It's 1:30 a.m. on Wednesday, March 17, 2015. I'm all alone in the cavernous hospital waiting room where I've shoved together three sizeable ottomans of hard burgundy vinyl. Because they refuse to accommodate my 5'9" frame, I'm curled up in the manner of a cat, holding tight to my body heat, trying to halt my limbs' inexorable slide over the edge, like spaghetti slipping over the rim of a colander. My carry-on suitcase stands upright like a sentry. I had packed in a hurry—a crazy person tossing in a baggie filled with almond butter slathered on crackers, organic walnuts, a thermos of my favorite green tea, my cervical bed pillow, my cellphone charger, Steve's wallet, his medical ID necklace, who knows what else.

Steve, my soul mate of 16 years, is now lying on a table in the operating room being prepped to receive a new liver. I'm calling upon every ounce of self-control I possess to breathe smoothly—in and out, in and out—nothing to worry about, just in and out.

It's been four years since his diagnosis of non-alcoholic, cryptogenic end-stage liver disease and a very long slog for him, and for us as he slowly deteriorated and had to relinquish a teaching job he loved. If you ever have a question about linguistics and the English language, Steve is your man.

Today is the day we've been waiting for, though not believing it would really come to this—the day his sick liver is being replaced by a newer, healthier model. Even though I know he's in the operating suite, nothing about it seems real. I'm playing possum with my feelings—fear and panic are not my friends. Steve and I grew up in the Midwest (Illinois, Indiana), where stoicism reigned and where sucking it up quietly was de rigueur.

After Steve's gastroenterologist informed him four years ago that he was suffering from end-stage liver disease and would eventually need a transplant, Steve told me, "I felt a cold white wave of fear flashing up from my toes to my head, thinking I was going to die." As the years of waiting wore on and his physical deterioration continued, he retreated into his usual dispassionate turtle shell, leaving me to manage the logistics of our impending move as well as our unacknowledged roiling anxiety.

Now that the day finally arrived, I confessed to him before the transport attendants came how scared I was to let him out of my sight. He simply shook his head, his brown eyes flashing, and said, "Let's just get'er done!"

Nothing more could I do when the two strong young men came to wheel him into the operating suite, and the doors hissed shut, leaving me on the outside. Nothing. Feeling icy and hollow, I wept as I traipsed into the empty waiting room and took a seat, hardly breathing. I'd read that liver transplant surgery is considered an "ultra major" operation. Were we strong enough to prevail?

The only advantage for me of having had an abusive father is that in order to survive, I had to toughen up. I lived in a neighborhood full of boys, including my older brother, where I learned how to throw a punch with one hand and a spiral football with the other. And outrun them all.

But will we be able to rise above the vicissitudes of Steve's transplant? This has to work, it just has to.

There is no Plan B.

Steve barely escaped death during his evaluation week here at this same hospital two months ago. Due to the negligence of the evaluating gastroenterologist, we ended up in the emergency room on our second day. The surgical resident who examined him foolishly decided to give him a shot of heparin, a blood thinner. He obviously had not read Steve's medical record. I am a former health care administrator, case manager, and psychotherapist and knew how dangerous heparin would be for Steve, who had only 30,000 platelets. Normal begins at 150,000. I stepped in and blocked the nurse from injecting him. I heard nothing from the doctor after that.

After I complained to our health plan coordinator at home about this near-fatal error and told him I was freaking out at the idea of bringing Steve back here for his transplant, he reminded me that the surgeons were excellent and that the patients they referred here had received good outcomes. He also informed me that our health plan had contracts with hospitals in two other states, and we were welcome to go visit them. Neither of us could have survived that sort of schlep. This has to work.

It's cold enough in here to preserve meat. I'm shivering under my black sweats and the pink fleece jacket I bought before we left California for this out-of-state hospital, thinking it would cheer me up. Why do hospitals have to be so cold? To keep the germs drowsy, is what I've heard, but who knows. More likely to save money. Hospitals have massive overhead to consider—must perform a lot of transplants to keep abreast of expenses. The combinations are staggering: liver & kidney; liver, kidney & pancreas; heart & lungs—miraculous pulsing bundles harvested from one generous gifter, to be flown here and installed into the welcoming viscera of a grateful recipient. We know nothing about Steve's donor—man, woman, where she lived, how he died, how many grieving family members she left behind, what he had planned to do with the years he thought he had left. We might never know.

A nurse, gowned in pale gray scrubs and hat, her mask dangling against her chest, had floated in on crepe-soled shoes to see me at 11:35 p.m. last night, to let me know that as Steve was being administered the happy drugs, he started spouting limericks. Perfect for St. Patrick's Day.

"Oh," I said, sitting up and reaching for my glasses. "I hope he didn't launch into his favorites."

"Yes, I'm afraid he did, but I know a few dirty ones, too, so we had a high old time." She laughed. I laughed. Just two gals in a bar, sharing a funny story.

That's my honey, I thought. Still talking. We've often joked about him being an out-loud linguist, one who loves nothing more than an overfull class of university students needing and sometimes wanting his wisdom about linguistics. I often tease him, "You'll still be talking even after you're dead, won't you, Sweetheart?"

She also let me know that Steve's surgery had been delayed thanks to the opaque killer fog shrouding the airport. The private jet conveying his life-saving liver has been circling round and round for the past thirty minutes.

"What if there's an accident?" I said, my voice quavering. "How much longer before it can land and be taxied to us?"

"This happens all the time around here," she said. "We're in a fog belt. No need to worry."

Easy for her to say.

At 1:45 a.m., the nurse has returned. No jokes this time. The liver has landed. Steve is doing well. I tell her that even though Steve is ill, he still possesses the natural constitution of an ox. All those years of childhood, working on the family farm in Indiana.

At 2:12 a.m., another nurse bustles out to tell me the surgeon has made "the cut." This is transplant speak for *we are slashing your husband from one side of his abdomen to the other*. My stomach clenches. The rubber is now meeting the road. It will be another seven hours before we know if this has a happy ending. I think about the donor's family. There is no happy ending for them. How do you grok that someone has to die so someone else can live? If I were religious, I'd feel a chill.

"Are you okay?" the nurse asks.

"I'm really cold. Do you have any blankets?"

"Sure." She pivots and scurries down the hall as if she's off to save another life. She returns with four heavy covers.

Three TVs, one in each corner of the waiting room, are tuned to the "Wendy Williams" show. Blah blah blah blah, *Spanx*, blah blah, blah blah, *Botox*, blah blah blah. I search for the "off" button but can find only the volume control. I reset it to low, but it's still too loud. My earplugs fail to keep the broadcast from laying claim to my mind, thwarting a craving to curl in upon myself, to shut out the babble. To dive down for one worry at a time, hauling it up to polish the rough edges like a gemstone until it's less likely to nick me and make me bleed.

Repeating the process seriatim, I struggle to make sense of the nonsensical.

Rosie Sorenson, MA, MFT, writes CNF, including memoir, political satire, and humor. Her work has been published in many outlets, including newspapers, columns, and anthologies. Her awards include the Joyce Turley Scholarship from the 2020 San Francisco Writers Conference for an essay; the Listener Favorite Award from the popular San Francisco NPR affiliate in its "Perspectives" series; winner in the essay competition from the Writers College, UK and NZ; Honorable Mention in the Erma Bombeck Writing Contest. Visit her on LinkedIn and at RosieSorenson.com.

The Black Box of Memory

By Suhail Rafidi

Zerqa, Jordan. 26 July 1956, Thursday.

On a sweltering summer day in a dusty village on the outskirts of Amman, a child was being born. It was a home birth in a small domicile above a storefront on a side street of the village. The house was sparse and practical, designed for airflow to make the most of the desert climate. It had airy rooms with high ceilings - plenty of room for cooking smoke, hookah puffs, and drying laundry.

The young woman in labor had married at age 12 and birthed her first child at age 14. This arriving baby was her tenth, and not to be her last. She was at an age we Americans consider the bloom of youth, her mid-twenties, and had been pregnant since puberty. She moaned in the bedroom. Sisters, cousins, and elders acting as doulas and midwives bustled about with linens, herbs, and hot water, coaxing her about the belly and loins, helping her adjust her position, and generally drawing her amniotic infant into the breathing world.

The men of the family sat in the front room of the house with dour brows, chewing their lips and chain smoking. The father was a butcher, dense of muscle and steady of nerve. His profession was an asset and a convenience. How else would he keep ten children well-fed, if he didn't own a meat shop, and bring home scraps and choice cuts? He and his sons, with concerned relatives and neighbors, waited for the new addition to the family. They were listening intently. Some were so intent, that their idle cigarettes sent squiggly ribbons of smoke to join the accumulating carbon monoxide layer at the high ceiling. Others puffed voraciously and exhaled like sleeping dragons through commodious noses. The room was never large, and it was crowded that day. At first glance, it may seem that they were concerned about the birth. They were present for the birth, in a manner of speaking, but it was trite and seemed to be going smoothly. Their concerns were most definitely elsewhere. They had drawn their seats into a tight circle around a small transistor radio turned up to full volume. The President of the budding republic of Egypt, Gamal Abdel Nasser, was addressing the Egyptian people, and, more to the point, the entire Arab world.

"These struggles in Jordan, in Syria, in Sudan, in Algeria, everywhere in the Arab countries, we cannot say that they do not concern us, because all of us, the Arab countries, are intimately linked to others, and we never accept that we follow foreign powers, that we receive our instructions from such and such a power..."

Cigarettes were snuffed into ashtrays, and fresh ones ignited in their stead. The men's hearts were filling with something, something they'd had difficulty feeling for a long time. But this man on the radio, he was calling to it.

The Suez Canal, connecting the Red Sea to the Mediterranean Sea, was a critical trade route on Egyptian soil. The vast majority of all the revenue generated by the canal went to England and France, with a pittance to Egypt. The young republic wanted to finance a new engineering project, the Aswan Dam. The dam would control Nile flooding, generate hydroelectricity, and generally catapult Egypt's industrialization to new heights. England and America backed out on a promise to finance the Aswan Dam, and Egypt's Suez Canal allowance wasn't enough to pay for it. So, it seemed they were out of luck.

"Poverty is not a shame, but it is the exploitation of peoples that is."

The men in the birth house in Zerqa, Jordan, knew this story, to varying degrees. They shared it with each other in snatches between puffs. Some shushed others for talking over the speech. If this speech means what they think it means...

"Who made you our tutors? Who asked you to mind our business?"

In the culmination of his speech, Nasser announced the nationalization of the Suez Canal, claiming it for Egypt, as it was in Egypt, and built by Egyptians. All of the canal's proceeds would remain in the country. Egypt could pay for its own damn dam, and buy its own guns, using its own canal.

"We will also achieve many of our aspirations, and will effectively build this country because there is no longer anyone for us who meddles in our affairs.

"We are free today and independent."

I fancy our Founding Fathers would have been proud of Nasser. He was talking to all the Arab people, and all the world was listening. By the end of the speech, the men in the birth house were speaking so simultaneously and so loudly that the radio was drowned out. That something which was stirring within the hearts of the listeners grew into a feeling and a vision. If the Arab countries got together from Gibraltar to the Arabian Sea, imagine their clout. Imagine their economic prosperity. Imagine their unit of currency running down any pound or dollar, or not-yet-existent Euro for that matter. Their future was so bright, the sheiks would wear shades. These rustic Jordanian men waiting for baby number ten were, like millions across the region, rooting for the tall, keen, bold Egyptian president. That vague, forgotten feeling stirring in their hearts was heated and formed, and waking them to a regal ancestral memory: Pride.

***

The cry of the newborn pierced the air, over their cheering and admiration. A weary midwife stepped out of the bedroom and made an announcement. The baby was born.

"It's a girl. What will we name her?" she asked the father.

There was no hesitation. The newborn's adult brothers clamored to their father. They were in a frenzy of pride and elation and called out the new name.

"Tameem! Tameem!"

"Tameem?" the midwife replied. "Are you crazy?"

But the men in the room were caught with the fever of freedom and power. They would not be dissuaded.

"Tameem! Name her Tameem!"

And thus she was named.

When Tameem was three months old, Israel, France, and England, according to a later-revealed secret plan, invaded the Sinai peninsula, land of Egypt and the Suez Canal. The three visiting countries issued an ultimatum to Egypt: surrender the Suez Canal. British Prime Minister Anthony Eden, on top of wanting control of the canal, wanted Nasser killed; or "deposed", as they say in history books. The international community was outraged. Opposition to the acts came from the home fronts, from the UN, and from Soviet threats of intervention. England and France got a whiff of the Cold War, and the fiasco ended. They immediately withdrew their troops and lost most of their flex in the Middle East. Eden was ruined and resigned shortly thereafter. It was the last nail in the coffin of England's colonial empire. Israeli forces lingered on the Sinai peninsula, finally leaving in March 1957, missing their chance at a Suez foothold. Nasser became a hero, an icon. The streets of Egypt were teeming with ebullient citizens celebrating their beloved, triumphant leader.

Tameem was eight months old.

Those of you who speak Arabic may be saying to yourselves: "How curious. Tameem is not a name, it's a verb." Correct: Tameem is a conjugation of the verb, "to nationalize" or "Nationalization." The midwife asked if he was crazy because it would be like naming your child, "Immunization," or "Configuration."

Tameem was born into, named after, a rushing current of Pan-Arabian pride and self-determination. Arabs were rejoicing from the Nile to the Persian Gulf. Her family fostered this pride in her at every opportunity as she grew from suckling babe to precocious toddler. She knew her name was unique. She knew no one else in the world had her name. When she was introduced to people, they nearly all remarked curiously after her name. She stood tall in her shoes, jutted out her chin with pride, and explained that she was named after the greatest day in history, "Tameem't al Canal al Suez."

Kamal, one of Tameem's older, university-attending brothers, wrote an adoring letter to Gamal Abdel Nasser, telling him how wonderful it was to see a strong leader draw Egypt and the Arab people into global influence. He told the story of Tameem's birth and naming, in honor of Nasser's brave, proud actions. Shortly thereafter, a letter arrived from the offices of the President of Egypt. The letter was a gracious thank you, and a humble acknowledgment of the child Tameem, and the hope and pride she embodied. With the letter was a special certificate, signed by Gamal Abdel Nasser. It guaranteed Tameem a full scholarship to an Egyptian university when she came of age to higher education.

She became the family's extroverted golden child, a talisman of possibility. She basked in this knowledge and shared it unabashedly. She grew to be clever, willful, and gorgeous.

Suhail Rafidi is a writer and educator whose works explore the destiny of human values in a technological landscape. Discover his work at suhailrafidi.com.

Jake at the Dump

By Tim Campbell

Mom steered our 1947 DeSoto down the dirt road leading to the dump in the small town of Fair Oaks perched on the far reaches of Sacramento. Dust billowed up from under the tires as she pulled into the helter-skelter parking area. My grandma sat up front with Mom. We came to a stop. Mom and Grandma paused for a moment, gazing around. I sat in the back seat, curious but not sure I wanted to be in this smelly, run-down place.

Mom said that Jake usually piled up rescued stuff for sale. She pointed to the corner of the lot where an array of items stood out by their still-visible paint and where no fires were burning.

The clicks of our door handles sounded, and the rush of hot air and alchemy of acrid odors smacked me in the face. I slammed the car door to keep the smell out and turned around to view the smoldering landscape. Nearby, leaves of pages in a telephone directory flickered with dying flame. Flattened debris—tin cans, broken shards of glass, plastic, cardboard—lay interred into the dust at my feet. Decades of trash formed small hills rolling off into the distance.

"Tim, you can't go over there," Mom said, pointing to an area past a row of tires.

"You don't know what kind of stuff you'll run into," Grandma added. "Glass, fire, rats, snakes." Her eyebrows arched high. I stood motionless, wondering where I *could* go.

The dump lay across large mounds of river rock. It was a desolate place, kind of at the bottom of things. Yet for my eight-year-old eyes, the few earlier trips with Dad to the dump proved that there was always something intriguing to find there—broken toys, radios, bikes - stuff that had been discarded on the edge of the city.

A tricycle with the smashed front wheel still had some red paint on the frame where tongues of flame hadn't yet reached. A set of old radios peeked out from beneath layers of ash and dust, the mystery of their exposed tubes and dials there for exploring. Like every other artifact at the dump, they seemed forlorn, having lost their purpose in life.

I heard Grandma say, "Hi, Jake, how are you?"

I turned and saw a man approach us. He made mumbling and grunting sounds, but no intelligible words. A crumpled, dusty hat covered part of his face, which was lean and unshaven. Tattered clothes carried generations of filth, his arms bare and hands worn, his beat-up leather shoes with loose laces seemed two sizes too big. His mouth hung open, and drooling spittle flowed over one corner.

I stared dumbly at the man. His jerky, uncoordinated movements made me uncomfortable. His twisted face and drool scared me. Yet, a faint smile was discernible.

He raised his arm toward Grandma, as though signaling a welcome, along with higher-pitched mumbling sounds.

"Hello, Jake," my mom chimed in, raising her hand in greeting, a warm smile on her face, as usual. Jake's eyes brightened as he turned towards Mom. His smile widened into a crescent. He lurched a step or two closer to us, but it could not be said that he walked toward us. His palsied gait carried him in a kind of ungainly way. I thought he should not try to hurry anywhere. I feared that he might overrun or collide with his destination.

Jake glanced at me, and our eyes met. He made a slight nod, his cattywampus smile still in place. He was less scary now, but I was afraid to talk to him, to make him feel as though he had to answer me, worried that I would have to answer an undecipherable mumbling from him.

Mom had told me that Jake had been at the dump for a long time. Dad and Mom and Grandma visited the dump from time to time to unload refuse from our two-acre parcel, where Dad pastured a few heads of cattle, a dozen pigs, and a coop full of chickens.

Mom said, "We're looking for a corner table, Jake." She paused, seemingly to track his understanding. "About three by three."

A flash of recognition lit Jake's eyes. He made another grunting sound, softer than the ones before. He turned and made his way in a slow, stumbling manner toward a pile of rescued items. He shuffled back, carrying a triangular table, and put it down in front of us.

My grandma said, "Pretty good, Jake." She indicated a spot near the car. "Leave it there... we'll look around a bit." Jake placed the table near the back of the DeSoto. Mom and Pearl began to peruse the for-sale area.

Tires lay in a semi-circle around things rescued by Jake. A broken lamp sat on a three-legged table. A dented stove rested next to a refrigerator without its door. A pile of books had been placed on a table, a vacuum cleaner stood at rest, its cord wrapped into a loop hanging limply from the handle. Scores of small items languished wistfully as if hoping for reclamation. To the rear, with its door open, a battered old house trailer, so dusty and ashen that its color couldn't be determined, looked like Jake's house.

The largest part of the dump consisted of an amorphous collection of refuse that couldn't be salvaged. Partly recognizable items stretched in scattered disarray over acres of undulating piles of rock. In those days, there was no landfill, no tractors plowing earth over layers of refuse. Fires nibbled away slowly at whatever was flammable. Sometimes they popped up spontaneously.

After a while, Mom hollered, "OK, Jake, I think we'll take the table."

Jake, who was sifting through the trash looking for items to bring to the rescue zone, lumbered over and came to a stop. He mumbled something unintelligible, but Mom and Grandma seemed to understand.

Grandma said quietly to Mom, "Buck and a half, seems like a lot."

Jake stared motionless at the two ladies. He lifted his hands and made a sign; his right hand hit the palm of his left hand.

Mom said, "Six bits." She looked at Grandma, who nodded.

"Six bits, OK," Grandma said.

Mom pulled out a dollar and handed the bill to Jake, who stuffed it awkwardly in his front pocket. "The rest is for you, Jake," Mom said.

Jake's smile returned.

Mom opened the trunk of the DeSoto. She lifted the table, but paused, seeing that it wouldn't fit easily in the shallow space. Jake then made more grunting sounds and, in a jumbled way, rolled his hands one over the other, indicating to Mom to reorient the table. Mom stood, hesitating. Jake came forward and took the table from Mom and, though jerky and awkward, fit it snugly into the trunk.

"Oh, thank you, Jake," Mom said. She smiled warmly, and she and Grandma bid Jake farewell.

Starting the car, Mom said, "It's sad about Jake. Must have been a birth defect."

"Yet he's intelligent," Grandma said. "Understands pret'near everything. Keeps the dump organized."

"All by himself… a broken-down trailer for a home… no family," Mom trailed off. Grandma looked down at the damp tissue in her hand.

I felt an ache in my heart and an urge to help as we drove out of the dump along the dirt road to the highway. I kneeled up to the back window and caught sight of Jake. He was organizing things, putting a little order in the chaos of the waste stream, seeking to squeeze a little more value out of society's discards.

He looked up. I waved. He raised his hand high, higher than I had seen before, almost saluting. An aura of dignity settled over him. He seemed to be standing taller, even as his figure receded slowly as we drove along the road out of Jake's world towards the highway.

Tim Campbell's personal narratives—about fatherhood, travel, and working with the poor in developing countries—have been published in various magazines and literary journals. He has written three professional books on cities and scores of articles on urban development. More can be found at TimCampbellOdysseys.net.

Adult
Fiction

Category Winner:
Young Men

By Lauren Domagas

The evening belonged to us now. Long ago, the little campers had been tucked away into their bunk beds. A tearful goodbye was to be had in the morning, but we, the camp counselors, still had the night, and we were trying hard not to think of summer's end. Together, me and the rest of the guys drowned out our thoughts in heat, sitting around the campfire, perching so close to it that it burned our marshmallows and surely our skin.

I surveyed my own marshmallow, rotating my skewer every few seconds over the smoke. Laughter spritzed into the air. There was a glow to everyone's round faces, a brightness made only in exaltation. The night had just begun, but my eyes were growing heavy, only to be struck open by a sudden movement across the fire pit. Jason, a fellow counselor, had leapt from his seat and was now sticking his skewer straight into the fire as if jousting with it. His marshmallow caught ablaze, and he snatched it away from the fire in one fell swoop. For a moment, he poised the fiery marshmallow in the air, a flash of rippling crimson and blue. He looked to the group expectantly, all his dare stacked up, before swallowing the flames and marshmallow whole. We all screeched out in horror, but just as quickly as it had begun, Jason stood beaming in front of us, sticking out his tongue in triumph. Unburned.

Most of us laughed out loud, a disjointed sound between terror and delight. We clapped, but Trevor, one of the older counselors, shook his head.

"Never do that again," Trevor said, frowning.

To that, Jason shrugged his shoulders. A grin had developed on his face, and he didn't want to lose that, but Trevor's words had had an effect on him, so Jason softened to quietness and faded into the background. He had all but disappeared before his eyes fell on mine —an expression I couldn't read— before plucking himself free from the group. After a moment, I went up after him.

Away from the fire, my skin burrowed against the sudden coldness as I followed him through the woods, toward the outskirts of the campgrounds. He swam through the trees without glancing back, having never been taught to wait. His pale neck would dodge between the shadows, though somehow, I was always able to find his neck again, even when I thought I had lost it completely.

We came to a cliffside that opened toward the ocean. I stood against the beating wind as salt air flooded into my nostrils and sand granules flew into my mouth.

"Young man, you're not supposed to be here," Jason teased when he saw me.

He sat on an ashen tree log and patted the area next to him. I took a seat, looking outward and absorbing the ocean. It was a magnificent sight: the ocean indigo-inked, with its dark beady eyes considering me back. I wondered what it would be like to lose myself to it, to lay my head down into its lap.

I shook myself alert. "You left," I said.

Jason smiled. "Confession time: if I'm not the most tragic person in the room, I leave to find a new room." His eyes queried me sidelong. "If you're wondering, you were the most tragic person tonight."

"Me?"

"Yes." He looked at me strangely, puzzled that I didn't know.

"What makes you say that?" I demanded, bolting to my feet. My fingers curled at my sides, and I wondered if this moment called for me to hit him.

Instead of answering, he stood up too, taking a long moment to brush his pant legs straight. Then he asked me why I had followed him. I didn't know what to say. I didn't have the words. How could I explain to him that it just seemed like the most natural thing to do? That if you counted him, I'd be right there. Wherever he was to go, I was sure to follow.

Instead, I kissed him suddenly, square on the lips. To my amazement, he didn't shy from me, inviting me to come closer with the soft pillow of his tongue. He tasted of weed, listless nights, and billowing smoke. Of open air and echoing unanswered calls. I kissed him hungrily to the point of devastation, like I might steal some of his vitality. I wanted some of it for myself.

It was Jason who pulled away. He stood a few inches back, smirking and intrigued. "You're braver than I thought," he said.

"You underestimated me," I whispered raggedly.

Jason dropped his chin, looking at me levelly in the eye. "I promise not to do so again." Then he took a step back, glancing down at the cliff's side. All at once, he seemed to be registering the steep drop, and he grinned, so widely that it revealed the cracks in his face.

"Do you think the waters will catch me?" He asked.

I didn't say anything, only watching him. I think it surprised us both when he didn't jump into the abyss that offered to swallow him up.

Lauren Domagas is a writer who blends cinema and novel techniques to explore human emotionality and the Filipino-American experience. She plans to self-publish a collection of short fiction stories, which includes 'Young Men.' For more information, visit LaurenDomagas.com.

Ghost Town

By Alex Tricarico

"I like it," Dennis announced, but quickly followed with, "I'm just afraid they won't understand that term." He frowned at the ad, verbalizing the word *term* as though they—Dennis and *term*—had an unpleasant history together.

"Which term?"

"Bullish."

"Bullish?"

"Yes. And it also looks a little like bullshit."

"Like...bullshit?" Apparently, I had left all my declaratory sentences back at my apartment.

"At first glance. Like when you look at something quick," he clarified, additional context to assure me that he wasn't, in fact, stupid. Too late. He looked at it again, squinting now as though failing a DMV eye test. "Yeah. Bullshit. Now I can't get past it." He said it once more to convince us of his inability to proceed unmolested. "Bullshit."

I wanted to ask if penises came to mind when he saw something about multiple pine trees. But this was a client, and I could only say these things in the privacy of my own suffering.

"Why don't you think they'd understand?" I asked with intense casualness, a preemptive strike against my face which I feared would rearrange itself into a rictus of malignance if left unattended.

"It's not something you hear every day," Dennis explained with a countenance suggesting what it was saying was perfectly reasonable. "Unless you're really into the markets."

I employed my inner monologue to test the soundness of the statement. *Unless you're really into the markets.* Fail.

"So," I began, trying to get things straight in my head, because my ears couldn't quite grasp what they were receiving and then—via various forms of biological voodoo—conveying to my brain, "our emerging affluent target, who are self-directed investors, won't understand?" I spoke in an exaggerated manner, emphasizing the situationally ironic phrase '*self-directed investors*' as though I were speaking to someone with limited intelligence, ending on an interrogative crescendo to underscore my incredulity. If I couldn't call him an idiot outright, I intended to vigorously imply it.

"Exactly," he responded with the face, my scorn slipping by unnoticed like a sneak thief.

I stared, wondering if he were one of those people incapable of reading social cues or situational context or voice inflection or bald-faced sarcasm or oozing irony.

"It's really the idea that matters. The copy is FPO." It was a voice of reason, a thing of which I was not currently in possession. Karolyn—my creative director—knowing I was about as capable of hiding my feelings as an infant with gas, swooped in to suture the meeting closed before the bleeding became unstanchable. I smiled. Karolyn smiled. Stupid smiled.

***

"You want to hit me," Karolyn mused aloud over half-caf soy vanilla lattes down in *The Annex*, our ultra-hip gathering spot littered with amorphous chairs resembling lava lamp goo writ large in ever-escalating shades of puce. An enormous flat-screen TV displayed an attractive talking head silently mouthing something about the latest bank failure while an endless stream of red numbers slid by below, ticker style, in eight-inch portents of doom. Apparently, the world was taking a flume ride straight down the shitter.

I glanced at the screen. The anchor was lovely. And smart. Even with the sound off, I somehow knew this. And she had really great hair. I suddenly wished that I had really great hair.

We were sitting at one end of a long table, hip quotient off the charts like the chairs. I checked my reflection in its surface, crafted from carefully randomly cut maple, oak, or some such wood and sealed to a blinding shimmer, likely by some swarthy artisan with tattoo and beard volume in equal measure. My face, below pixie-cut hair, spiked just so, was blurry, as though I were viewing myself through a window streaked with rain, making it difficult to tell whether I was man or woman. *A nice little metaphor there,* I thought.

Karolyn eyed her latte. "I'm not really getting vanilla."

"Yeah. What?" I was absently wondering if I should've gotten a full decaf. Caffeine makes me poop. "I'm just happy there's something in my cup," I said, staring at the contents like an oracle reading entrails to determine whether heading into a battle with cannibal barbarians was an okay idea. Our touch-screen coffee machine, made of brushed aluminum (a very hip metal), was the size of a small car and spoke several languages while murdering beans through a convenient viewing port. In my many trips to *The Annex*, this was the first time it had been operational.

The Annex was where all prospective employees were interviewed so as to demonstrate that a century-old bank could be just as cool as the tech companies with whom we were competing for talent. When we failed to even convince *ourselves* of this, we added a seltzer machine with 27 flavors. Apparently, there was a high correlation between coolness and beverage diversity.

You want to hit me. This was how Karolyn always diffused my rampant indignation, whether she was smoothing over a client meeting, like now, or defending herself for not liking something I had written.

"A little," I said, my face mopey.

"Oh, Eeyore!" she exclaimed, extending her lower lip in pretend sympathy and honest mockery. This pet name had been bestowed without a hint of irony. "The clients are under tons of pressure. The metrics are killing them, and they need results, so they're scared of their own shadows. Any decision could be their last."

"Yeah," I extra moped.

"So they don't make any." It was true. My recent client meetings were less like meetings and more like séances, the clients trying to channel the ectoplasmic spirit of a decision-maker farther up the food chain for a whiff of how they might respond to a piece of creative.

Karolyn raised her palms in supplication, ten digits all crying *Help me help you.* She didn't like it either, herself having as much patience with most clients as a fat kid in a pastry shop, but as a member of the agency leadership, was contractually required to act like a grownup.

"Will shoes help them hit their numbers?" I, however, had no such limitations. But I knew I would lose this fight. I knew this because I lost every fight but always made sure I went down swinging wildly, like someone in a dark room who hears a threatening sound somewhere *over there.*

As the senior writer for the in-house advertising agency of *The First Bank of the Frontier*, I had the privilege of writing for our high-net-worth audience—a perpetual reminder of my low-net-worth status. Our most recent campaign featured a beautiful, affluent family (rich people weren't allowed to be ugly). The initial shot chosen was of a couple and children looking like they were straight out of central casting for a Leni Riefenstahl film. We needed more diversity, so, it being Asian American Pacific Islander Heritage Month, I suggested an Asian family. A nice tie-in, it was roundly acknowledged, however not diverse enough. The client wanted a mixed-race couple with appropriately hued offspring, a veritable racial dessert sampler, all within a conveniently packaged single nuclear unit.

Was I thrilled we were embracing diversity in our advertising? Absolutely. As a marginalized transgender member of our increasingly xenophobic society myself, I was a hearty endorser. And it was the right thing to do. And it was the smart, businessy thing to do. Underserved customers represented millions in revenue and would feel considerably more comfortable with a bank that not only acknowledged their existence, but their inalienable *right* to exist.

But this is what tends to happen in corporate America when a hot-button issue arrives via the CEO's newsletter or is mentioned as a "priority" during a quarterly fireside chat. It starts off admirably enough, but before you know it, the notion gets shanghaied by the eager-to-pleasers and gotta-save-my-jobbers, and militantly pumped to within an inch of its good-intentioned life until it eventually becomes a parody of itself.

In the photo, the members of our family were holding hands in descending order—a perfectly diverse human charm bracelet—strolling down a pink beach, the sand glowing as though absorbing the fierce energy of the sun and meting it out to each member in turn with a soft halo effect, one more blessed than the last. The client, however, felt that bare feet, like senses of humor and contractions (the language kind, not the birthing kind), were decidedly *un*affluent and therefore shouldn't—sorry, should not—be present. People of a certain economic stratus, apparently, were dour, spoke like an Edith Wharton novel, and wore loafers to bed.

"You gotta let the no-shoes thing go."

"I know," I said (not meaning it), embarrassed (only a little), of my clinging to lingering resentment over petty offenses. *Letting it go* for me meant cataloging it away in my own perverse Dewey Decimal system from which I could instantly extract it at a later time when I felt infantile histrionics were appropriate to the moment.

Alex Tricarico spent many years as a copywriter in advertising agencies from Madison Avenue to San Francisco before jumping to the worlds of technology and finance. A former United States Naval officer, they hold degrees in finance and law. Coming out as transgender and nonbinary in 2021, Alex seeks to tell the stories of their community. They can be found on LinkedIn.

Neighborly Conversations

By Anna Marie Garcia

October 2000

Chapter 1: The Call

Shifting in my chair, trying to get comfortable with my book, the mid-morning silence was interrupted by a familiar knock. "Coming," I called, moving slightly slower than usual. I opened to my neighbor Lisa's relieved smile.

"Okay, I'll admit it, I was a little worried when I hadn't seen you in a few days," she said.

"I pulled a muscle in my back doing yard work. Probably hauling the branches I pruned. It's much better, though."

She had me sit while she made us Jasmine tea and pulled shortbread from my cookie shelf. "Have you met the new neighbors?" she asked as she filled my cup.

"Well, that's almost funny. I saw them going into their house last week, so I tried to see if I could pay the boy to do some yard work."

"How'd that go over?"

"Strange. The mother acted like I was a criminal. Sent the boy in the house, said he wasn't available to work for me and abruptly followed him inside. I didn't even get her name. Have you met them?"

Lisa said her encounter had been similarly odd. She took a cake over Saturday to welcome them and explain the neighborhood watch program. The woman stepped outside and closed the door behind her. Gave her first name, Rachael, but no last name. She hesitantly turned over her home phone number but made it clear it was only for emergencies, not to be added to any lists or given to anyone else. "Skittish and distrusting, I'd say."

"Maybe she'll warm up after she's been here for a while," I said. "What do you want to do about giving me her phone number for the child watch roster?"

Not wanting to breach trust, Lisa said she'd have to think about it, then asked when I was last watching the street. I easily remembered it was Friday morning because I hurt myself that afternoon.

"Tracy called me Monday evening," Lisa continued. "Her daughters ran home out of breath after some man yelled, 'Hey girls,' out his car window and motioned them over. They didn't get a car description, but Tracy alerted the school and drove them both ways Tuesday. She was somewhat concerned when she hadn't seen you out and about. Unfortunately, Tracy works today, and my lovely, dependable daughter Shelby has a late class, so she can't pick them up either."

I assured her I was good enough to sit outside on my porch after school. Said I'd call Tracy to tell Gabi and Vanessa to come to my house if they were scared and would let the school know if I saw anything suspicious. Lisa shared the neighborhood's appreciation, then hesitantly handed over the new neighbor's number.

"Promise, I said, "I won't call them to chat."

"Make a list of the yardwork you still need finished, and we can talk about it on the weekend," she said as she put her oversized China cup in the sink before letting herself out.

That afternoon, fall decorations up and down the street presented like artwork against the contrasting sky as their shadows danced. Scarlet and crimson foliage scattered at their bases as Gabi and Vanessa walked home from school. They waved at me from across the street. I watched them unlock their front door and go inside. A few minutes later, they called to let me know everything inside was fine and they weren't scared. My back was starting to throb, so I went inside to continue my watch from a more comfortable chair.

Before I even sat down, I saw a man I didn't recognize driving slowly down our normally tranquil street. His head smoothly swept side to side as he surveyed the scene. I reached for my pad and pen but couldn't see his rear license plate and didn't readily recognize the generic-looking make of the car. I watched him until he turned the corner, noting the car was forest green and he was wearing glasses.

To my right, I saw the boy next door approaching from about five houses away. He glanced towards my porch, quickly looked right and left, then focused on his front door. Despite his bulging backpack overwhelming his youthful frame, he maintained a quick pace. As he neared his front door, I noticed the green car had circled the block. He slowed and discreetly watched the sandy-haired boy enter his house.

He parked in front of Lisa's two-story house and sat there for a moment, focused on his steering wheel. My trembling hands reached for the phone list, as my stomach started to knot. I knew the girls were alone in one house, the boy alone next door, and no other adults home nearby. I wasn't sure if I should call 911 or wait to see what he was going to do. He looked out the driver-side window straight at the boy's house. I didn't hesitate. I called 911, gave a brief synopsis, and dialed the neighbor.

"Answer, come on, answer." The machine beeped on, and the best I could do was speak to the recorder, "Hello, this is your next-door neighbor, this is an emergency, please answer. You are in danger. Pleeease Pick UP! A suspicious man in a green car has been driving through the neighborhood. Come on, answer. He followed you home, I saw him. I'm trying to protect you." The answering machine clicked off without an answer. I redialed.

"He's coming up your walk. Don't open the door. DO NOT OPEN THE DOOR!"

"Hello. Who is this?" The youth finally answered the phone.

"I live next door in the blue house. I try to watch out for the kids in the neighborhood."

"I'm not allowed to talk to the neighbors."

"Don't open, he's at your front door."

"Why are you calling me? How did you get my number? My mom thinks you're weird and nosy. She told me to stay away from you and not talk to the old lady next door."

"I understand, but this is an emergency. I already called 911, and the police are on their way, but I want to keep you safe," I said as calmly as I could muster.

"Why? How do I know you're telling me the truth?"

"Because you're a kid, and I'm a retired teacher, and I watch out for children. I really am trying to help you. Believe me."

"I'm not a child. I'm twelve. Who's the guy?"

"I've seen him drive through the neighborhood. I think he's a predator. . . . Good job not answering the door. He's walking around the side of your house now. Get to a place he can't see you. Closet, counter, anywhere, quick," I directed, inching towards the rear of my house. "He's looking in the side window."

"I'm down behind the kitchen counter," the boy said, his anger waning and his voice fearful.

"Good. Stay there until I tell you, then get as close to the front door as you can. Stay low and away from the windows."

"Did you really call the police? Is this some crazy old lady game?" He questioned. His rapid breathing audible.

"I'm trying to help you. Now. Go to the front. He's not looking inside. He's scoping out the back of your house and your backyard. Get to the front of the house. Stay low. Don't try to look out the window."

"Should I lock myself in the bathroom?"

"No bathroom. If he gets into the back of your house, I'll tell you, and then I want you to run out the front door. If he doesn't get in, I'll give you other directions. The police should be here any minute."

"How long? Why aren't they here? Did you really call them? Is this a trick?" he questioned.

"I told them to get here fast. The man just tried the back door, and then he reached up and cut your window screen with a knife. I think he's looking for something to climb on because he couldn't get up to the window. Do you know if the window's locked?"

"I don't know. I'm scared. Are you sure I shouldn't lock myself in the bathroom?"

"Since he's trying to get into your house, I think we should get you out of it. Do you understand?"

"My mom told me not to talk to you. She thinks it's strange you sit outside when kids walk home from school. AND you're crazy."

"LOOK," I said, "I'm 68 years old and four feet eleven. Who's scarier, me or the man trying to get into your house?"

He took several short breaths, "I, I, thought I saw a man watching me yesterday. He creeped me out."

"He's standing on your garbage can and trying the window . . . it just opened. Are you near the front door?"

"Yes."

"When I say now, you open your front door and run to my house. My door isn't locked. I'll meet you there."

"I'm scared."

"You can do this. I'll beat that man myself if I have to. I will NOT let him hurt you. He's halfway in the window. NOW. GO. RUN TO MY HOUSE!"

Anna Marie Garcia is a fiction writer, poet, and world traveler. Her creative inspiration draws from personal experience: dancing flamenco on a baroque castle stage, paragliding above Queenstown, welcoming sunrise atop Mt. Fuji, and trekking the dirt roads of third-world countries. Living half of her adult life outside the U.S., she now calls the Pacific Northwest home. She can be reached at AnnaMwritenow@gmail.com

Written All Over Me

By Duygu Balan

Anthony

Thursday, September 18

I'm struck with the intense urge to flee. Strobe lights pulse behind my eyes. Everything is simultaneously muted and enhanced—the bookshelf filled with fake plants and magazines; the vagina-inspired O'Keefe flower hanging beside a row of framed empty words: *Courage, Wisdom, Hope.* Someone rips open a bag of chips, and I startle. Then I sit, and like every other person in this waiting room, I fuck around on my phone.

How was practice? I text my brother.

Jamie replies instantly: **Fine. Just got home. Where you @?**

Starting therapy. Finally getting my head checked.

He's the only reason I found the balls to show up here, but I don't tell him that part.

He writes: **Mom's losing her shit on me.**

She's probably drunk, probably shrieking that if he doesn't clean his room, she'll throw everything he owns down the trash chute in the hall. I try to come up with a plan, but all my options weigh the same and cancel each other out.

Dude, jump on the train and meet me at 59ᵗʰ and Columbus. I'll be out by the time you get here. We'll grab something to eat, then head home together?

Ok.

Now I feel even worse because all I can offer Jamie, who's probably sweaty from soccer and starving, is a choice between our drunk mother and an hour-long ride on the subway.

I pull a *Psychology Today* from the shelf. On the cover, "arrogant, witty, smart," and other descriptors are scribbled over a woman's face with a sharpie beside the headline, *What Your Face Reveals.*

A door opens, and a girl floats out.

When she shoots a quick glance in my direction, I see that her eyes look like the sea, gray and wet. I take in her paint-splattered Converse, the canvas messenger bag strapped across her chest and crowded with pins. The *We can't hug kids with nuclear arms* pin reminds me how much I hate humans; how we've invaded the planet and messed everything up with our cell phones, Wi-Fi, and machine guns. The book pins—*The Little Prince, Alice in Wonderland, Don Quixote*—make me think of Jamie propped against my chest, listening to me read. A lump expands in my throat. I decide to ignore the yoga pins. When she adjusts the strap of her bag, I see that her nails are painted black.

A man with a thin nose and square glasses brushes against her shoulder and says, "Excuse me." He beelines to the water fountain and fills a cone-shaped cup with the one drop of water it can hold.

The girl wipes her eyes with her sleeves, purple-black streaks smearing her face. I grab the box of tissues from the shelf and hand it to her. Our fingers touch. I swear I hear violin music.

"Sorry." That's the first word she says to me.

"Ezra Katz?"

My name tears into me like guitar feedback. I turn. Mona is older than she looked in her picture on the website, with frizzy blond hair with some whites. She scans the room, then her eyes land on me. I tense, but her eyes are so warm and wise, I relax.

Right before I walk into her office, I glance at the girl one more time. She's looking at me, too, a tissue in one hand, the box in the other, the saddest, sweetest smile I've ever seen shining through her tears.

Mona gestures to the couch. "Welcome, Ezra."

"I go by Anthony," I say. Then I plop myself on the couch and sink deeper than I anticipated.

She sits in a chair across from me. "Good to meet you, Anthony."

Her face made me think she'd sound soprano, but her voice spools out in a low octave with a husky edge. If she were to sing, she'd sound like PJ Harvey.

On the wall behind her, two brass puppets face each other, as if in conversation. I imagine Mona extracting them from an archaeological site in the Middle East. The likelihood of the puppets being bubble-wrapped and delivered by Amazon Prime makes me look away. When my eyes find their way back to Mona, she is watching me like an affectionate moon from a children's book.

"What brings you here today?"

Last week while I was making coffee, *Que Sera* by Jose Feliciano, a song Mom used to sing, traveled from a nearby open window, and my heart started thudding in my ears. When I shut the window, the amp inside my head turned the song up full blast, and then the record started skipping and glitching, looping and scratching on the same beat, on repeat. My vision got hazy, and then I threw up in the kitchen sink. By the time Jamie got home from school, I was still zooming in and out of childhood memories. When he realized I couldn't register a word he was saying, he looked at me with disappointment mixed with pity, the same way he looks at Mom. I guess he thought I was drunk. I was supposed to drive him to his game that afternoon, but I couldn't.

So that's what brings me here today. But instead of telling her that, I make a dumb joke: "The train."

Mona's earrings jingle when she laughs. "How are you feeling right now?" she asks.

I wonder what *my* face reveals. I scratch my chin and say, "To be honest, a little uncomfortable."

"Yes, of course, you're here knowing you'll be talking about yourself, and I'm a stranger. It's very natural to feel uncomfortable at first. This is a relationship that we'll build gradually. Over time, the room will feel safer."

The word "safer" makes me flinch.

"If I had a magic wand," Mona says, smiling, "and therapy worked wonders, what would be the outcome for you?"

I imagine Jamie on the train, playing a mindless game on his phone, looking like any other teenager—at least to strangers who don't know the truth.

When I don't answer, Mona tries a different question: "What would you like to work on?"

"I'd like to make my mind a better place to live," I say.

"Huh." She clasps her hands on her lap. "Can you help me understand what that means?"

"I have a lot of anxiety." I straighten my back. "I guess everyone does. But, like a few months ago, I was asked to tour with this ska band. It would've been a great opportunity. But I got anxious and turned it down. I do have a pretty steady gig now. And if I'm handed the notes, I got it, but if I'm asked to compose a sample, add a guitar riff or lyrics, I buckle. Recently we've been playing a song I composed, and every time I either feel like the piano riff is too simple or the verses are dumb."

"Are they?"

"Probably not, no." I feel myself blush. "In an ensemble, lean riffs work better, actually. And the verses are just conversations I have in my head."

"Ok, just making sure." She laughs.

I laugh, too, feeling momentarily at ease before I'm suddenly out of breath, and terrified by my own thoughts. I try to focus on the crashing wave sounds coming from the white noise machine. "Lately, I've been feeling like I'm going to make a giant mistake that'll dictate the rest of my life."

"Oh." Mona furrows her brows. "Whose voice is telling you that?"

I see Dad glaring down, his upper lip curled in contempt. "Mine."

Mona purses her lips. "I don't think so. Threatening voices that talk down to us don't come from within. They only seem to because we've internalized them."

I hear PJ Harvey again and start strumming the chords in my head for *Rub 'Til It Bleeds.*

"Let's get curious about these voices," she says. When I don't answer, she cocks her head to the side. "What happened when I said that?"

"I got anxious."

"Can you describe what that felt like in your body?"

"My rib cage got sort of tight." Fear spreads in my gut like molten tar. "Look. I don't really want to get curious. I just want it to go away."

Mona nods slowly. "Yes. That's very understandable. Often what gets in the way of healing are thoughts and feelings we've been avoiding. It takes time to feel safe enough to look at everything."

That word again. *Safe.* I think of Jamie and take out my phone. "Sorry, my brother's supposed to meet me after this." I slide the phone back into my pocket. "Just checking to see if he got here."

She smiles. "Are you the younger or older brother?"

"I'm both. I have an older sister and a younger brother. My little brother's still a kid." My voice cracks.

"Your little brother's still a kid," she repeats, looking straight into my eyes.

"Fourteen."

When Mona glances at my leg, I see that it's shaking. I press my hands on it to make it stop.

Duygu Balan worked as a clinical counselor in New York City, treating patients on society's margins. She is the co-author of the best-seller *Re-Write: A Trauma Workbook of Creative Writing and Recovery in Our New Normal.* She is currently a contributor to *Psychology Today.* Born in Germany and raised in Istanbul, Duygu's upbringing provides her with a fresh perspective on how to navigate tension between cultures. You can find her @duygubalan on Instagram or on her website DuyguBalan.com.

The Switch, Inc.

By Eliza Mimski

-1-

"Our first pair of Before and After photographs show a thirty-year-old Caucasian man who went through the switch and is now Filipino," Valentina said to a group of eleven patrons who were mostly white, the rest Asian, and as far as she could tell ranged from their twenties to their sixties, all but three of them women, and for the most part a respectable-looking, well-dressed group in sports jackets and ties, pantsuits and dresses, all except for one disheveled twenty-something guy in ripped jeans and a T-shirt that hung askew from one shoulder, a denim jacket over one arm. She gestured toward the huge backlit Before photo mounted on the wall showing a nice-looking young Caucasian man with red curly hair, pale eyes, and a heavy physique who in the After photo was a slightly-built Filipino man with jet-black hair parted on the side, his face wide, a flashing smile showing off a dimple on one cheek, his serene dark eyes giving off what was known in switch circles as the *RLOF*, or the *Relaxed Look of Relief*.

"How long has he been Filipino?" a female patron with long dark hair asked, she herself seemingly Filipino. Valentina replied that it had been a little over two years, and she wondered how this woman felt about the man's switch. Some races were flattered when others wanted to join their race, while others saw it as an invasion. Or, maybe the woman herself was a switchee?

Valentina fingered the lanyard around her neck. *Ms. De Guzman, Tour Director and Guide.* "The four questions that people are required to answer before their switch are: *From what age did you feel you were born into the wrong race? How has this manifested in your life? What are your expectations in terms of how your life will change? What is your life like now?* "The Caucasian man in the Before photo had known from the age of six that something wasn't right about him," she heard herself reciting. "He only felt at home in the company of his Filipino nanny who'd raised him, and the older he got, the more he felt a part of that culture and at odds with his own. He'd hoped to find some inner peace after his switch, which he stated that he did. He now lives a full, happy life."

Many of the patrons nodded, seemingly impressed.

"What's the process for one becoming a switch candidate?" a short, roundish woman in a red dress asked. The woman was built much like Valentina, who today wore a short red wrap with a V-neck that tied across her midriff, outlining her stocky figure. Valentina still wasn't used to this new body of hers, only having inhabited it for the past six months. Although she didn't go around thinking of herself this way, it was true that people often found her sexy. One random man on the street had recently referred to her as a peach. Another had called her juicy.

Becoming a switch candidate. The woman's question was one Valentina anticipated as someone invariably asked it on every tour she'd given. She never knew if the patron was asking out of curiosity or had a vested interest in the answer.

"That's a great question," she said, and she ran her hand through her long wavy hair that was an ocean of black waves. "Let me just say that each candidate goes through quite a lengthy process before they enter the Switch Room." She rattled off the process, all the way from the psychological evaluation by a team of experts, to therapy with a psychiatrist trained in this area, to a support group led by a past switchee, such as herself, all of which helped them to understand what to expect as they entered the world as a racially different person.

Valentina led the group from one room of the exhibit to the next. She showed the group more of the Before and Afters, one of a white woman who had transformed into a Native American and one of a middle-aged white man who had become a Pacific Islander. She answered more questions, such as how costly the switch was, replying that it was estimated to be over three hundred thousand dollars. The patrons' eyes widened at the cost, but then she explained that large corporations offered grants one could apply for. When would people be able to switch to a different age - yet another question - to which she replied that this was currently being worked on. As usual, the older patrons seemed to be paying special attention to her answer. Someone else asked about switching to a different gender, and Valentina explained that in today's liberal world of acceptance, folks weren't asking about that so much.

So far, the tour was like any other tour she'd led, and Valentina was relaxed and confident. "How does someone acclimate to the new culture?" a man in a brown sports jacket who had a thin brown mustache asked. "Do they just learn it bit by bit, pick it up as they go along? And what about language? Does everyone who switches races in the United States come out speaking English and nothing else?"

Valentina, in her usual professional way - she'd gotten her calm exterior this go around with her transformation - explained that during the switch, the client was instilled with a cultural background of their new race plus the ability to speak standard English and any language used by their culture, such as Spanish, Tagalog or Mandarin. All the information was implanted inside of a disk, but she was not allowed to say this because issues of one being controlled would no doubt come up, and this was a tour, not a debate.

"Well, it sounds like one way to learn another language quickly," said another patron. "A lot faster than Babbel."

Valentina was glad for this light-hearted comment.

"Can you switch back to your original race if you're dissatisfied?" someone else asked, and she responded with a no. Even if they could, she thought, no one would want to go back to an identity they felt the need to escape from. Once you switched, she told the small group of patrons, there was no turning back. What she didn't mention was that you would go into shock and die if the disk were to be removed. "You could, however, switch to a new identity." She'd switched twice and still wasn't happy, so why would she want to switch a third time? What would be different? When another patron asked if you remembered who you once were, Valentina told them that at first, you shared a co-consciousness with your prior self, but after a few months, it became harder and harder for you to remember your prior life, and then your memories faded away, and this was why the company provided each upcoming switchee with what was called a Remember Journal, a large brown leather-bound book with a lock and key so they could record important information about themselves that they didn't want to forget.

"What exactly happens in the Switch Room?" someone else asked. Valentina smiled. It was well-publicized that organizations that performed race-switching, such as *The Switch, Inc.*, or *Asian Reincarnation* which originated in Tokyo, or *Black Is Beautiful and You Can Be Too* that was owned by a group of Black businesswomen in Chicago, or even *Lighten Up to White* that was located in Alabama - the organization never really getting off the ground - guarded their secrets in this highly competitive, emerging field of the last twenty years.

"As you know," Valentina replied, "the switch does not involve plastic surgery of any kind, and short-term memory is erased during your switch. In other words, no one who exits the Switch Room remembers the process." All Valentina could recall was a spinning sensation and then everything going dark.

"Does The Switch perform transformations from darker races into the white race?" a woman asked.

Valentina shook her head. "I'm afraid we don't do that here," she instructed her. "However, there is a company in Alabama that specializes in this, and if anyone shows an interest, we refer them there." She noticed a disgruntled look from the young guy in the jeans and T-shirt, the denim jacket now thrown over one shoulder.

"Do you think the people who do this stuff are just crazies with emotional problems?" he asked. "You know, like, what they really need is a good psychiatrist?" He was rumpled-looking, had a slow, smug smile and messy brown hair, and his intense eyes gave her a challenging look.

The air in the room tightened. Valentina glanced at the burly security guard in his dark shirt and shiny company badge. She hoped the patron could control himself and wouldn't have to be removed. Narrowing her eyes, she looked at the obnoxious guy through her long spidery eyelashes. What an ass, she thought, but she stood up straight and kept her professional cool.

Eliza Mimski is an educator living in San Francisco, California. Her work, including poetry, flash fiction, short stories, and personal essays, has appeared in print or across the net. You can read more of her work at ElizaMimski@wordpress.com.

Author's Helper

By Jason T. Small

After cocking the gun, Diego pulled the trigger. He knew it was a good shot because the bullet had already hit its target two hours earlier.

I stare at that sentence on the screen in front of me. "Man, that's a good opening line," I say to my computer. Unfortunately, I wrote it three weeks ago.

Frustrated that I have been unable to write anything since then, I spin around in my chair as if trying to get away from the screen. On the shelf behind me are my two Sci-Fi Novel of the Year statues from more than a decade ago. I put them right behind me as a reminder of how good I used to be.

Hi. My name is Jeff Nulty, successful author of six sci-fi thrillers, including the Damian Ellison series, and I can't write anymore. Last week, I was at a writer's conference talking to one of my editors, who wanted to help me. "I understand what you're going through," he said excitedly. "You have to see this new website, Jeff. It has helped several writers."

He then borrowed my laptop to open up a website called Author's Helper.

"What is it?"

"It can help with ideas. You just type in what kind of ideas you are looking for, and it will write something for you. The writers who use the site swear by it. They use what the website spews out to get moving on their story."

"Wait, a minute. Is this an AI writer?"

"Well, yeah," he said sheepishly.

"No, no, no. Did you not watch *Terminator 2*? That's how it starts. If we let an AI write stories, it will soon be dropping bombs on us."

He just shook his head at me and then showed me how it worked after opening a guest account with my name. He typed, "A lone gunman runs through a forest" into the prompt on the webpage.

Within moments, a story of several thousand words pops up.

"*War and Peace*, it is not," I said dismissively after reading it. I was using my snark to hide my disappointment because it was actually a pretty good story.

Since then, as the unwritten novel remained stuck on the first paragraph, I constantly thought about how easy it would be to get the AI to help me restart. So far, I have resisted the temptation, but my resolve is crumbling.

Another day has sped by, and nothing new has been added to the novel. The idea of using the AI keeps nagging at me to the point I just want to shut my mind off.

With midnight already past on another failed day, my eyelids are fighting to close. I should just pack it in for the night and admit defeat. With my defenses down, my resistance evaporates.

"Fine. Let's just get it over with."

Without thinking, I go to the Author's Helper website.

What do you want me to write, the screen asks me.

Operating on autopilot, I activate my computer microphone. The question stares back at me.

"I don't know," I say aloud. "I just need a new novel. This is killing me."

Letters pop up on the screen, but I'm too tired to read them. I decide sleep is more important than some AI.

With my bed beckoning, I slam the laptop lid down and forget about it.

***

I sleep poorly, yet again. After a few hours, I get up out of bed and stumble down to the kitchen.

I make myself a coffee before sitting down in front of the computer.

"Today's the day. I will write a second paragraph." I don't even sound like I believe it.

I open the laptop. There is a wall of text on screen.

"Did I sleep-write? Is that even a thing?"

Before I can answer myself, I see the computer is open to the Author's Helper website. I scroll down and see the writing goes on and on.

"Oh no, Skynet wrote a novel."

I go back to the top and look at the story's title.

Killing Jeff Nulty.

How does it know my name? I then remember my friend at the writers conference. He had put my name into the website.

"Nooooo. That's how they get you," I cry out.

I should delete the story and get away from this website. Instead, I can't help myself.

"You're weak," I say, but I start reading anyway.

"I guess I have to save the world again," Damian Ellison muttered to himself.

"Yuck," I say aloud. "That is a horrible opening line."

That's when it hits me - bad writing is not the issue here, it's the fact the AI used my own character for the story. This is too weird, but I need to know what it says, so I keep reading.

After the cheesy opening line, it turns into a strong first chapter. Damian discovers a rupture in the multiverse that could destroy his dimension. He quickly realizes that he must go alone to a different dimension to stop the person who is causing the rift.

"I know who has torn through the fabric of our dimension," Damian tells Elana. "His name is Jeff Nulty."

Even though my name is in the title, it's still weird to read it coming out of Damian's mouth.

Further down, Damian steps out of a copy of *Gravity's Shadow* (my sixth and least successful novel) and into Jeff Nulty's world.

"This makes no sense."

"Doesn't it?" asks a voice from behind me. I jump in my seat.

As I spin my chair around, I am greeted by the barrel of a Luger P08. The hand holding it is connected to a tall man with tanned skin, a thick head of brown hair, and a good physique. He's wearing a black leather duster over a faded Iron Maiden T-shirt and blue jeans. I've never seen this man in the flesh, but I know him well.

"You look like Damian Ellison."

"I am Damian Ellison."

"You can't be. He's not real. He's only in my head."

"Not anymore. And no, you're not dreaming. The new novel has opened a rift between our dimensions."

"What new novel?"

"The *Killing of Jeff Nulty.*"

"But that's not a real story. It was written by an AI, not me."

"It has created a rift between our dimensions. I need to undo the damage of that rift before I can return home."

The title of the story comes back to me, and that's when I realize that Damian plans to kill me to repair the rupture between dimensions.

Shaken, I think about how I can stop him. I pull myself back to the laptop and start furiously typing right after the part where Ellison arrived in this dimension.

Damian realizes Jeff Nulty does not need to die. The rupture was created by a sentient and malevolent computer hellbent on destruction, not Nulty.

I turn back, hoping that the man has vanished.

"Do you think you could be more cliched than 'hellbent on destruction?'" He's still there, the gun still raised.

"I wasn't going for quality."

"Maybe that's your problem."

"Of course that's my problem. My writing sucks now."

"I don't have time for your self-pity. I have a dangerous man to stop."

"But I'm not dangerous. It was the AI."

Ignoring the pistol, I turn back to the screen. I read on in the story to find something else I can change to keep him from pulling the trigger. Then, another name appears.

Damian has to find Arturo Jacobian, who also stepped out of one of Nulty's books. Ellison has to prevent that murderer from wreaking havoc in this world, creating a permanent rift between the dimensions.

"Jacobian is here, too?" He is the greatest villain I have created. He's Moriarty to Ellison's Holmes. And if he's here, he could destroy the real world.

When there is no answer, I look up. The gun isn't in my face anymore. My front door is wide open. I look out the window to see the man in the duster running down the street.

I now know he wasn't calling me a dangerous man. He meant Jacobian. He is off to find the arch-villain, and I am left wondering if I've lost my mind.

A few minutes ago, the two characters were just creations of my once fertile imagination. Even though it makes no sense, I know this is not a dream or hallucination - an AI has somehow made them real.

I go to read what is next in the AI's story, but I stop.

"No. I am still the writer. This is my story to write."

With that, I run to the door, slide on my sandals, and head for my car. Somehow, I have to find these two, stop them from damaging the real world, and get them back to where they belong. I'm going to do that without a computer's help.

Jason T. Small is a fantasy and science fiction writer based in Winnipeg, Manitoba, Canada. For more on his writing journey, go to JasonTSmall.com.

Compliance Setting

By Melissa Geissinger

Lilly takes a last sip of wine and puts the glass on the counter before traipsing seductively across the apartment to where Gregory sits on the couch, waiting. The apartment's lighting dims automatically to fit the mood, anticipating her romantic intentions. She climbs on top of Gregory, straddling him against the cheap synthetic IKEA upholstery. Gregory caresses Lilly's cheek with the back of his fingers gently, just how she likes it. He kisses her gently on the lips twice, then crams his tongue down her throat while pulling her close and flipping her onto her back, just how she likes it.

Lilly fumbles for the button on his pants as Gregory gropes her breast. Gregory sits up on his knees and reaches for his zipper. He holds still for a moment before asking her, "Do you consent?"

"I consent, I consent!" Lilly screams.

Gregory unzips his pants, throws himself back on top of her, and kisses her deeply.

"I just heard about a deal at Safeway," he says.

"What?" Lilly pants, perplexed. "Not this again."

"USDA Choice Ribeyes are on sale for $32 a pound. Should I add some to the grocery list?"

"Sure. Yes. Fine. Just keep going!"

Gregory unbuttons his shirt at lightning speed, removes it, and throws it behind the couch.

"I've added it to your shopping list," Gregory pulls Lilly closer.

Lilly sighs and pushes Gregory away. "Gregory, go open another bottle of wine."

"Are you sure, muffin? You've finished one bottle already, and the last time you drank two, you woke up with a headache."

"Yes, I'm sure! Now do what I say!"

"Yes, Lilly, anything for you." Gregory dismounts Lilly and walks toward the kitchen, where a corked bottle of Alexander Valley Pinot, vintage 2032, waits for him.

"Oh, Gregory?" Lilly yelled after him. "What is your current compliance setting?"

"Compliance is currently set to 72%," said Gregory as he picked up the bottle opener.

"Set compliance to 80%."

"Yes, muffin."

Gregory freezes for a moment. His eyes turn glossy and opaque while he updates his system. He resumes his motion three seconds later, popping a cork.

"Yay!" Lilly squeals with delight.

"Will you keep it down, Lil? I'm trying to study," I interject.

"Calm down, Nora. It's just foreplay."

"Can you at least turn the lights back up? I can't read my notes."

"Why don't you do us all a favor and take your Conga Neuro-whatever books back into your room where they belong."

"Cognitive Neuroscience," I sigh and collect my books and my papers that are strewn across the dining room table.

"Whatever. Nobody cares about this robot you're trying to build anyway."

"Well, someone cared enough about it to have my mom killed for working on it."

Gregory hands Lilly her glass, now full of blood-red pinot noir.

She takes a big gulp and then smacks her lips. "Didn't they conclude she died of natural causes?"

"Yeah, electric car batteries blow up randomly from *natural causes*. It was her life's work developing AI therapeutics that made her a target. It threatened the very purpose of these damn MatchBots. Heaven forbid people actually learn how to work through their problems rather than running to a glorified butler sex doll."

"MatchBots are not, in fact, sex dolls," Gregory announces, raising a finger in protest.

"We are synthetic humanoids designed with sophisticated personality matrices that can intelligently adapt to our partner's personality type and moods. Our purpose is to measure and predict our partner's ideal match so that they may one day find their—"

"Shut up, Gregory," says Lilly.

Gregory obeys.

"And honestly, Nora, it's about time you grow out of this little rebellion phase. It's completely normal to have a bot partner. Literally, everyone does. And if you don't, you just wind up like that crazy old homeless man that talks to himself."

"First of all, don't talk shit about Frank. Frank doesn't talk to himself; he stands on the corner in the town square and invites everyone he meets to his birthday party. That guy's my hero. Secondly, you get that it's not a real relationship, right? It's just a mirror reflecting yourself back. Or a shadow of the person who took care of you when you were young. In the end, everyone just ends up in some messed up relationship with an unattainable version of themselves or their parents. Freud would have had a field day."

"Ew, Nora," Lilly shakes invisible muck off her hands. "I'm not in a relationship with my dad. That would be sick."

I stare at Gregory's blonde hair with patches of gray to make him appear distinguished, as Lilly puts it. "Yeah. Nevermind. How could I ever say something like that?" At first, I worry she heard my eyes roll, but then I decided I don't care if she hears me sound upset. I don't even want to hide it anymore.

"Why are you being so mean to me?" Lilly asks.

"You're just . . . you're just not the same person you used to be, Lil. You think you can order me around just like you do with Gregory. I don't have a compliance setting. I'm a person."

I gather the rest of my things and walk into my room. As I close the door, I hear Lilly fumble with vocabulary.

"I, um, eh, fine . . . Leave, then! If you're going to—"

The door slams shut.

I set my phone down on top of a docking station at my desk, and spokes of blue light of varying lengths radiate from a holographic display port behind the phone, throwing harsh blue light into an otherwise dark room.

"Computer," I say aloud, channeling my best Geordi La Forge or Dr. Beverly Crusher.

"Open all files pertaining to my thesis project."

Each of the eight iridescent beams ends in a bright rectangular spot that simultaneously expands into the outline of a semi-transparent floating screen. Then, one at a time, each virtual display renders a different program.

While my screens all load, I take a moment to clear my desk from the week's worth of accumulated coffee mugs and dishes that have piled up. I look around for a place to put them all and just slide everything over to the side of my desk.

My research glows all around me—various charts, graphs, VR simulation data, and multiple windows full of interviews. I grab my black-rimmed augmented reality glasses from off the desk and put them on. Each of the displays now appears three-dimensional and moves with a parallax effect reacting to my movement.

A notification comes up in the corner of my holo-display. It's a memory from twelve years ago—June 17, 2023. Curious, I pinch to select it, and a video starts playing of Lilly and I learning a stupid dance for a TikTok challenge when those were a thing. Retro music plays from the 1990s, and we're side-by-side wearing blindfolds as we dance. A caption overlays the video that reads, "Seeing how similar we dance." Social media was so weird back then. I study Lil's face. She's smiling from ear to ear, and it's so . . . genuine. We must have both been thirteen. I miss her laugh. She was so happy. And I was happy. This was a couple of years before my parents split. God, I can't remember the last time I was that happy.

I close the window containing the memory and reach out and grab one of the windows with the interviews, move it in front of me, and begin flipping through them. I come upon one titled "Subject 12," make L shapes with my fingers and use them to enlarge the display. I pinch my fingers together and press the floating Play button to begin the recording. A transcript appears on the side of the video.

I hear my recorded voice ask, "Daniel, can you describe your experience with your MatchBot?"

Daniel says, "Yeah. At first, it was amazing. Sara, my MatchBot, was so sweet. Over time she learned all my favorite foods and looked up recipes on how to cook them for me. She knew just what to say to make me feel better after a long day at work, and she even knew, well, you know. How to perform. It felt like I'd found the perfect partner."

"Then what happened?"

Daniel's eyes break contact with me and flutter around as he shifts in his seat. He sighs and looks at the floor. "Things were just . . . too perfect. So perfect that it wasn't authentic. It wasn't real. Nothing changed. There was no challenge, no growth. It was like living with a mirror that only reflected what I wanted to say. There was no unpredictability, no partner with their own problems, issues, or accomplishments to celebrate. It just . . ."

"How did that make you feel?"

"Empty."

The recording ends. I melt into my chair like a used-up candle. I worry that will be Lil one day—empty and alone. I have to help her before it's too late.

Melissa Geissinger is predisposed to following her dreams and every side quest along the way. Her debut novel, *Nothing Left But Dust*, was published in April 2023. Proud mama to a 5-year-old heart warrior who, like her, is driven by curiosity, she injects adventure into their lives at every opportunity. She's a content designer at H&R Block, a fire survivor, and a serial entrepreneur who enjoys wandering the wilderness with a camera whenever "lifey stuff" gets too overwhelming. You can follow her writing, both UX and creative, at MelissaGeissinger.com or on Instagram @melissageissinger.

The Last Real Radio Station in America

By Norman Charles Winter

I have an insecure wife. She says she loves me. Nevertheless, she just locked me out of the house and suggested I go to Hell.

Why? I've been fired from seven jobs in eighteen months. It's not that I'm a lousy worker. I'm a great worker who sizes up the problem and goes about trying to fix it. Problem is, my *bosses* are lousy workers who talk about the different meows of their cats or whose superhero can wallop the other guy's superhero, with absolutely no understanding of the fact the American political arena is about to push the non-wealthy over the cliff.

Love is forever. But it has a bad habit of leaving the realm of forever when your consciousness realizes, "I'm not here anymore." It might be just as well. If I stayed, my consciousness would be spewing out senseless muck. So, the "forever" is *there,* and I'm over here with a bunch of homeless people in a cement, campground in Polihale.

Polihale Beach Park is a massive sand dune on a little island in the Pacific called Kaua'i. The island itself has a weird connection to other worlds that the rest of the planet is deprived of, and Polihale is at the ass end of that island. It's a heavy place of pathos swallowed in a deep rich beauty with blaring ocean waves that pound against godly mountains.

Why do I say godly? The mountains look like two-thousand-foot totem poles with the faces of Gods carved on their tops. It is here that the lives of the Earth exit into other worlds. I know that sounds crazy, but it is a perfectly natural concept to the people of Kaua'i. And you can feel the exit of life as the waves beat against the two-thousand-foot totem poles of the gods.

People call me a radical, which they misinterpret to mean I'm incorrigible, a rebel who is out to destroy their security. A radical, however, is a person that sees the problem and tries to find a way to fix it before the same people face a disaster that obliterates their security. I thought I could fix it in the business world, but here I am in Polihale, realizing the problem goes deeper. The root of the problem lies in the Constitution of the United States of America.

What does a radical do when he's faced with changing the Constitution of the United States of America? This radical drinks a beer, shouts out a few blasphemies to his friends or anyone who will listen, and then conveniently stuffs the disaster into the back of his mind. Some radical.

I realized at age sixteen: radio is the way to change the world. Why? It's a *sound-alone medium.* You hear a sound, and your mind imagines the visuals that go with the sound. It excites your imagination. You hear music, and your emotions are activated by the sound-alone medium. If a DJ's voice sounds sincere, a warm intimacy between you and the DJ is felt. It's like you and DJ are in a room together. If you hear listeners talking on radio, you feel more a part of the radio world. If radio opens the door to all kinds of music and ideas, you feel a part of the world, listening to radio.

My theory at age sixteen was that with radio, you are stirred into actively listening and feeling part of the world. Your consciousness is suddenly wired to the world, and you are a part of the whole, sharing your feelings and ideas with others. When enough people share ideas with each other, it becomes a snowball and ignites the whole world with motivating thoughts. Yes, utilizing your imagination in the midst of being a part of the world - that is a way out of the pit the world has put itself within. Radio could be the world's savior.

Now, I'm reconsidering. What does a sixteen-year-old know?

But then again, love won't save the world. Sorry, John Lennon. Love is forever and a great fix-it, but it wilts when consciousness yells, "I'm not here anymore."

Money won't do it. Sorry, Rockefeller. Money attracts the uncooperative people who work harder to get it so they can do whatever they want, and what they want is to shit on the cooperative people.

Religion won't do it. Sorry, Pope. Pledging allegiance to the invisible might make you feel better because it can't talk back, but when people get into a group and decide everybody has to think the same, imagination is crushed, and the larger the group, the worse part of the human nature ascends to the top.

Politics won't do it. Same problem. The larger the group, the stupider it gets, and political systems are huge.

So I came to the conclusion at age sixteen: radio is the best way to change the world.

When radio was vibrant in the thirties, forties, fifties, and sixties, didn't Orson Wells' "War of the Worlds," and Hitler's fanatical, emotional speeches combined with Churchill's emotional speeches, and the Beatles crushing the rigid views of the time leading to the Woodstock concert - didn't they all change the world?

If you were there, you know radio certainly did change the world. Of course, now radio is a limp rag you can't even wring out. And the culprit? I already mentioned that. It's the Constitution of the United States of America.

It's cold out here on the beach, and the wind just blew my belongings and my tent into the waves. Sand is stinging my face and blowing into my eyes, and I am beginning to believe Kaua'i people are right: this is where the torture of the earth's life departs. The trouble is, a whole bunch of that life must have been blasted dead in some war or terror act, and its departure isn't too soothing. Yeah, and it is a six-mile hike back to the main road, and then I've got to hope for the mercy of a speeding car zooming along in nowhere with this questionable visibility.

Here I am, Mr. Nature, trying to rough it without a car so I can think the deep thoughts, like what is my place here on this planet amongst the planet's natural surroundings? Stupid. What was I thinking? Coming out to the wild surf without even a car? And three nights from now, here in Kaua'i, I've got to meet my stupid ass words head on. What have I gotten myself into?

But there are cars here in Polihale. I'll take shelter under one until it decides to leave, then beg for a ride if it can tread out of the sand and find the main road in near-zero visibility.

I slither under a four-wheel drive, but it is still cold, and the wind and sand seem to find me there anyway. I cover my head with my shirt as the sand burns my belly. I hear noises, humans squealing, and some yelling verbiage, people shouting to others in a group. I assume they are saying to each other, "Get in the car, quick!"

I hear pots and pans clanking against the cement alcove, preparing to head for the ocean, and the tarp roof of the alcove is flapping loudly over the howling wind. The car rocks a bit and the engine starts.

Oops. Dumb idea, getting under it. But it doesn't move. They just turned on the heater. I should get in the car.

I belly crawl out and knock on the door. The door opens. "You poor man, you don't even have a jacket, jump in."

I hesitate. The front is a two-seater.

A girl pulls me in anyway. She's a pretty one, and the driver looks like a Don Juan. In the back are two glassy-eyed young men, one with dreads, the other with dirty sandy-blonde hair and a snarled beard.

The girl puts her arm around me, "Don't take it wrong, I just want to get you warm. My name is Mandy."

I'm out of her league anyway. I'm pushing fifty. "Hey, this is the best welcome I've had in a long time, thank you!"

Mandy is beautiful at second look: a full figure, bronze flesh, probably a mixture of a thousand cultures and races, and her brown eyes seem to flash into amusement, then solace, then a dreamy, distant look. When her eyes are dreamy it is like she isn't even there. I know that look, it is the sign of intelligence as if, why am I here? I belong somewhere else.

Now she smiles like she is the sun itself.

Damn, I wish I was younger!

Mandy says, "Are you one of those lost ones looking? Show me your hand. I read palms. Left one first; that's your past."

I show her my left.

Don Juan says, "She's really good, you know."

I'm trying to figure out why she thinks I'm a "lost one."

Norman Charles Winter has self-published two books, wrote two screenplays, one of which made the quarterfinals of both the Austin and Atlanta film festivals, and currently has a novel, *Beauty Star*, the story of a living star from another universe who has sacrificed herself to Earth to help save Creation. He has adapted *this* story into a musical with 18 self-written songs. Currently, he's the owner of a book and music store, Ideas Music and Books, in Honolulu. NormanCharlesWinter.com

Strange Ground

By Tracy Marie Oliver

Chapter 1

Pegasus Grace Monroe. That's technically my name. Yes, Pegasus. Thanks to my mother, a perennial new-ager. It's Peg, thank you, period. Brass tacks, just the facts, Peg. Smartass, first in my class, Peg. Youngest director of the San Francisco FBI field office, Peg. Fast track to Washington DC, Peg. I checked the navigation on my phone. No signal. I flicked on the headlights of my Pathfinder and stared into the distance. Only thick stands of evergreens lined the highway.

So how did I get here, banished to the wilderness? Oh yeah. I wished I could forget almost as much as I wished I could remember. I could squint into my memory far enough to see up until a point when four hours or more vanished, erased clean, as if a section of my memory had been edited. I only knew the fallout from that night led to a fast track to the middle of nowhere. I was now working the only two state area without an actual field office—Idaho, and Montana—known in the San Francisco office as Dumbfuckistan. It would be nearly two years before I'd be eligible for a transfer. A Paleolithic span of time. That's what I get for confiding in my boss. A mistake I vowed not to make again. The quiet time will do you good, he'd told me as if he were doing me a favor.

I checked my phone again. Still no signal. I was looking for a farm an eighth of a mile or so beyond the ten-mile marker. Deep hillbilly country. Where was the GPS signal when you need it? I missed practically everything about San Francisco except the exponential rents.

I'd lucked out on my place in western Dumbfuckistan, a Montana milk house turned cottage overlooking a pond with swans and wild geese. I'd pay a fortune for that in the Bay Area. The bungalow was next to a barn-turned-art studio that was never used. The cottage and studio were nearly a football field away from the great house that was also never used, not as long as I'd been there anyway, since April 1st, that's right, April Fool's Day. It was already June. According to the caretaker, this was just one of many properties owned by David Forrester, a man I'd never met but whose name I often heard whispered by passersby in town. I was the new girl in Trout Creek, and apparently, it was big news that I rented one of the Forrester properties.

Add to that, my features are exotic enough to evoke speculation about my heritage— a mix of a white mother and an uncommonly tall Asian man. I never knew my dad. I got preggers with Peggers and we flew to the stars, Mom is fond of saying. According to my mother, his only redeeming feature was his looks.

I spotted the highway mile marker and the farmhouse beyond perched on a low hill surrounded by pastureland. They called it a highway, but it was only a dirt road that led far up into the Rocky Mountains, where it turned into a logging trail.

My tires popped over gravel as I headed toward the farmhouse. I thought it was a girl who stood outside by the garden gate, hugging herself in her arms. As I rolled to a stop, I saw it was a woman, small, maybe middle-aged, but girlish in her oversized sweater. A grey pit bull panted by her side. I stepped out of my truck and introduced myself as a field agent for the FBI. Lately, the field had been behind a desk tracing the interstate internet trails of meth traffickers. I was grateful for a real field and took in a deep breath of air and the scent of alfalfa grass and cow manure.

"Maria Cooper?" I eyed the pit bull. The pit bull stopped panting and eyed me.

The woman nodded. She'd reported a spat of livestock mutilations on her property which wouldn't have been unusual if didn't mirror a case investigated by the FBI over a half-century ago. I surveyed the surroundings, a humble farmhouse amid a rolling expanse of alfalfa meadows where cattle grazed in loose pods. I doubted this place had changed much since the 1970s. Beyond the barbed wire was dense forest. These cows were sitting ducks.

"I know what you're thinking," Maria said. She sifted through the pockets of her cardigan and pulled out a pack of brown butt cigarettes. "I've been around livestock herds all my life. I know what it looks like to lose an animal to predators. Nature looks natural." Her cigarette bobbed in her mouth as she spoke. She flicked a plastic lighter. It only sputtered and sparked. "I don't know which is worse. No cigarettes or cigarettes, but no fire."

I tried to look sympathetic but was relieved to avoid second-hand smoke in my hair. "I'd like to get moving before we lose light." It was almost dusk. I used to call it the golden hour in San Francisco. It was different here. This is the time when things eat other things.

Maria took the cigarette from her lips and motioned with it in the direction of a corral. "Down there." She patted the dog. "Bonkers, stay."

The dog still stared at me with yellow eyes. "Do you need to lock him behind the gate?"

"Don't mind him. We don't get many visitors out this way. Not usually anyway" Maria walked toward the corral, and the dog stayed behind.

As we neared the scene, I noted a heaviness in the air. Not a birdsong or an insect buzz. Only the sound of caution tape wrapped around a fencepost flapped by a dry wind. A remnant of the county sheriff's office investigation that afternoon. It was the sheriff who raised the flag to the FBI. Though the FBI case from the 70s cited animal predation, even after 50 years ,the local ranchers weren't buying it. I'd anticipated this visit to be more of a public relations move than an investigation. Now my gut said different. This could be interesting.

"Not even the crows will touch it." Maria stopped and looked down at the hollowed-out carcass. "Poor Suzie. She was our milk cow."

I almost flinched. I caught my breath and squelched the impulse to step back. The skin around the nose and eye socket was absent as if the animal wore a flesh-colored mask. I dropped to my haunches to get a better look. The skin appeared removed with digital precision. The exposed flesh void of any visible red blood cells.

"What did I tell you?" Maria said. "No animal did that unless it was handy with a laser beam." She pressed her cigarette to her lips and gave the lighter a few futile strikes.

She has a smartass quality to her, I noted. "When was the last time you saw poor Suzie alive?" Part of my job involved making the FBI "more relatable" to the Dumbfuckistanis.

Maria wrapped herself tighter in her arms. "Wasn't all that documented in the sheriff's report?"

"I'd like to hear it in your own words if you don't mind." And listen for consistencies and inconsistencies. I looked up and caught Maria in an eye roll. My PR approach wasn't working.

"I was out in the garden all morning, and Suzie was in the pasture. I didn't hear or see a thing until around noon when Bonkers started howling up a storm. That's when I knew we lost another one. No animal tracks. No human tracks. Just like the others." Maria stared at what remained of Suzie. "It was a sorrowful, pitiful howl out of Bonkers. He and Suzie were the best of friends."

I sniffed the air around the animal's hollowed-out nose and eye socket for traces of chemicals that would explain avoidant scavengers. No, but there was something else. It was as if the air was heavy, less oxygenated. What would cause that effect? I considered the options. A cauterization tool?

"Cautery would stop the blood, not drain it." Maria said.

"Hmm, I wondered the same thing." I stood and moved to the rear of the cow. The rectum and sex organs appeared to have been hollowed out with the same bloodless precision.

"What did I tell you? Maria said. "Nothing natural about that. This is the third one in as many weeks." She stared beyond the pasture in the direction of the dense forest. "It's that summer all over again."

There was a gravity to her words, as if she had direct knowledge. Could she be old enough to remember?

"Oh, I remember," Maria said.

I did the math in my head.

"13," Maria said. "I was 13 that summer."

I stared hard at Maria, whose gaze was still fixed on the forest. It's like she knew what I was thinking.

Maria tried to light her cigarette again, and it sparked. She inhaled so hard it made my lungs hurt. She tilted her head and exhaled the smoke into the sky. "Took you a while. Longer than most."

I froze. "Okay, this officially just got weird." She was kidding. Right?

"What did I tell you when you first drove up?"

I replayed the scene in my mind…Maria, by the garden gate, wrapped in that big sweater looking like a girl. Not a woman in her 60's.

"I've always looked young for my age. I thought it was a curse back then. Now it's a gift. Funny how that works." She snubbed out her cigarette on the fencepost and returned the unsmoked portion to her pack. "I quit, just not today." She turned her gaze back to the far woods. "I suppose I wasn't the only one who felt cursed that summer. The whole town fell under a spell. That poor old widow bore the brunt of it. There's just no reasoning with blind fear. Fear and reason live in different realms. I've learned that much on my time on Earth."

I tried to track two conversations. Maria's story and the conversation in my head. The first words out of Maria's mouth were, I know what you're thinking. And what am I thinking now? I tested.

"Part of you thinks you might be losing your mind, which is a good sign that you're not." Maria cocked her head. "The other part of you is having a hard time swallowing that it took you longer than most to figure out the nature of things on this backwoods little patch of hillbilly country."

I was stunned. She'd nailed it.

"Well," Maria said, "I hate to break it to you, but truth is truth. There's just no improving on it. Welcome to Dumbfuckistan."

Tracy Marie Oliver is a writer and award-winning mixed-media artist. Her written work has appeared in *Room Magazine*, *Contrary Magazine*, and on KQED, San Francisco's NPR affiliate. She lives in Santa Cruz, California, with her two cats. TracyMarieOliver.com

A Red Book

By Wendy C Wong

Zhong Ji Ming recited the numerical coordinates to himself until he could find a safe place to write them down for his son. The safest place, he finally concluded, was in the pages of his Little Red Book. It was 1966, and millions of copies had been distributed. They were everywhere. Everybody had one. Worn and earmarked, always within reach, a badge of loyalty to the Struggle. A salve, a magical mantra. Reciting from Mao's Little Red Book eased every kind of pain and suffering – even the pain of childbirth. Women in labor read from the Little Red Book to distract themselves. Men undergoing surgery – with acupuncture as the only anesthetic – brought along a copy of the Little Red Book as a supplementary painkiller. Perhaps it was written precisely to numb the mind.

Like a book of prayers, many did not even need the physical book. Every verse had been so deeply imprinted into their memory most everyone could chant its lines forwards and backwards.

Zhong Ji Ming had transferred to the math department a few years before the Struggle began. He had wanted to study physics, but in his generation, physics was a field dominated by foreign dogs who had unleashed a kind of destruction that could never be undone. Oppenheimer had invented the atomic bomb, and China was directing its most promising physicists to secret teams to develop its own atom bomb. Ji Ming did not want to weaponize his passion for physics, so he steered himself toward mathematics. He was proud to be an academic like his father, a respected university professor; the right choice, that is, until the Cultural Revolution, when intellectuals everywhere became suspect.

The year before, Ji Ming had married his sweetheart, the daughter of his own high school physics teacher. They were starting a family, and they named their only son Zhong Tong Xin 鐘同心, meaning of the same heart. To fend off trouble, they declared their loyalties to the Party publicly and often, but none of that mattered; Ji Ming had a class problem, and it was only a matter of time before he would be sent to a labor camp in the countryside, set up to re-educate intellectuals into proletariats. His father, a historian, had been one of the preservationists of ancient relics for government-sanctioned museums and archives – which on the one hand, gave him honorific status since certain national treasures were so valuable and precious that even the Party condoned protecting them for posterity; but on the other hand, made him suspect, since historical relics were symbols of obsolete traditions and old dynastic power structures. His father's scholarly reputation was a double-edged sword.

As a preservationist, the elder Zhong had access to an official archive, and he understood its cataloging system. Well before the Struggle formally began, he had managed to stow away a special book with a red cover belonging to his own family among the national treasures – an almanac that had been passed down from generation to generation, which documented almost five hundred years of the Zhong ancestry. It was the Zhong Family jia pu, the official family tree that the first-born son of each generation was to steward.

The elder Zhong had taken great risks to hide it because it traced their ancestors to imperial oracles. Once a source of prestige, the tides were turning. Officially, only the descendants of Mencius and Confucius were allowed to preserve their family genealogies. Yet this lineage was potentially even older. It was far too dangerous to keep something so rare and precious in his possession. Red Guards searched every neighborhood, overturned drawers and mattresses, and seized anything and anyone going against the mainstream.

Putting his special privileges as a preservationist to use, he wrapped the Zhong Family jia pu in archival paper, and placed it into a nondescript carton, then cataloged it with other official relics to keep it safe. He marked it as "Shang Dynasty" – the first and oldest dynasty in China – confident that this legacy was too precious for even the most adamant party official to contemplate destroying. Then he noted the carton's location with a set of official government-assigned numbers – an archival number that would accompany the longitude and latitude. Someday, he hoped that his son would be able to retrieve the jia pu.

He understood the China he knew was being wiped from memory, but he hoped that this family history might survive.

"As a historian, I can attest that this is the darkest time of human history. Be careful, and stay alive," the elder Zhong told his son as he took his last breath.

Ji Ming held his father in his arms and wept. He would have to turn himself to stone in order to face the coming days, but in these extraordinary times, even stones were moved to tears. 石破天驚 shí pò tiān jīng. Something so astonishing was unfolding across China that even the Heavens watched in shock.

Under his breath, Ji Ming whispered, "Forgive me, Ba, for what I must do to survive. You know that my loyalty belongs forever to you and our family."

He knew that he could not give his father a proper burial. The Red Guards would take his father's body. To protect his wife and toddler son, they would publicly show their fervent devotion to the Party, and they would renounce his father in public.

That night, he spoke to his wife, whispering the plan in the dark. It was the only way: she would raise their son like a model revolutionary, and ensure that no one could ever question his loyalty to the Party. Ji Ming copied the string of coordinates and numbers into a clean copy of Mao's Little Red Book as a farewell gift to his little son.

Only a few days later, as expected, Ji Ming was taken into custody. Not only was he punished for being an intellectual himself, he was to repent for his father's alleged crime: anti-proletariat practices for conducting genealogy research of China's greatest emperors. Such family ancestry records were considered elitist fixations by rightist landlords and the wealthy class. The Red Guards had begun a campaign to burn all genealogy documents, including the ones preserved in village temples. By the end of their campaign, some 800,000 family jia pu had been burned and countless temples destroyed.

Ji Ming was sent to a re-education camp, where his job for a full five years was to dig up family graves to aerate the land into farmable soil. A punishment dreamed up by sneering bureaucrats. His sentence would have been far worse if his historian father had not been prescient enough to hide away their own family jia pu, or if they had learned about his illicit smuggling of artifacts. But for Ji Ming, this punishment was far more than back-breaking manual labor, which began before sunrise and ended after sunset; this was a psychic punishment, the ultimate shame. To violate the burial grounds of village after village was a crime against the sanctity of family, against the ancestry of an entire people, and the skulls and bones he uncovered haunted him for the rest of his life. He had no choice but to follow orders day after day. Like everyone else, he numbed himself by reciting from the Little Red Book. And when he became numb to the work, he was sure that he had turned into a monster.

Ji Ming's wife and son were spared. She adhered to the plan, openly denouncing her father-in-law. Her chronic asthma kept her in administrative jobs in the city. As agreed, she raised their only son to never challenge the status quo, even when they were treated like outcasts for his father's "crimes." Conformity overshadowed every other impulse. The boy grew up not knowing how to discern his own voice from the echoes of the official posters pinned to public walls.

On his annual visit home, Ji Ming matched their Little Red Books side by side as a symbol of their connection, reciting the identical numbers he had inscribed into each of their copies. But this boy did not want to know the secrets of this stranger he called Ba. The long stretches of absence had taken its toll. Zhong Ji Ming could not win his young son's affection. He grieved for his country, for his own father, and he grieved that he could not win back his only son. But for his crimes of disturbing the dead, he hardly believed he deserved a different outcome. Not knowing what else to do, he clutched his Little Red Book.

Wendy Wong writes about Asian American identity, family, ancestry, memory, forgetfulness, and the loss of ancient wisdom traditions in her fiction and creative nonfiction. This piece entitled "A Red Book" is excerpted from her novel-in-progress called *Soon*. You can find her on WendyWong.Substack.com, where she explores the human condition through the archetype of Evelyn Wang. Her newsletter is Everything, Everywhere – The Best Version Yet.

Poetry

Category Winner:
Tumultuous Trails

By Daniel Moreschi

An arid highland's time-worn slopes and humble views
of meager plants and cacti framed by sandy hues
are slowly wrested of their luster; gloomy shades
assume the heights, just as a gust-borne sweep pervades

a range to rouse a brown eruption and a stone-
filled whirl. A torrid downpour follows and is blown
across a foothill; like a famished wave, it soars
and swallows mountains to the tune of echoed roars.

Between terrains of screes and clefts, a run of thrums,
above a gully, but under summits, rumbles and becomes
its own refrain amid the wails of gales: a herd
of mustangs maneuvers through a hail-draped haze to gird

a mesa's sprawling contour, forming wanton lines
against the tempest's might. The way ahead declines
and veers, but still they stay. A sudden lightning flash
is met with stop-start steps and nodding heads, while a lash

from the onset of thunder entices their strides.
They charge at the elements, flooding the sides
of a canyon with blankets of eddying gold,
enveloping every rupellary fold.

On reaching the passage's perilous heart,
their gallops meander, unravel, then part
as far as the channels allow. They surpass
a release from a shattering cliff, but a mass

continues to plummet at startling speeds
and blows up in clusters that cover the steeds.
Despite being cumbered, they clamber; they wade,
and outdo the tumult with battle cries, frayed.

They rise in the race with the valley's collapse;
emerging from billows and narrowing gaps
as they mirror the rage of the wind and the rains
with the sways of their tails and the blaze of their manes.

They turn into blurred undulations in streams,
propelled by the pelts of their hooves on the seams
and gravels that crackle and crack where they swarm
the wide-open spaces to see off the storm.

The blasts are outlasted. The eddies abate
—above and below— as the tremors grow late
and the skylines and ridges no longer ignite:
a tenuous truce for a day and a night.

The weary horses settle down; they strut around
a playa. Though the peaks are fractious and the ground
is mostly barren, without fields or woods to roam,
this setting is their solitude. A sanctity. A home.

Daniel Moreschi is a poet from Neath, South Wales, UK. After life was turned upside down by his ongoing battle with severe M.E., he rediscovered his passion for poetry that had been dormant since his teenage years. Writing has served as a distraction from his struggles ever since.

abuela?

By Ángela N. Solis

it's always a long wait, with a lot of people, and a lot of noise.
a temporary space that feels like it holds eternity, i remember every stain on the wall, every chair that is broken.

i'm still restless, but instead of the pattering of my once tiny feet
across the room, my heart now races in its nervous rhythm
and i hold Mami's hand tight as i sit beside her.

i rub my thumb on her protruding veins and i wonder how
many times she had to grip the broom as tightly as she
does for the first one to etch itself across her hand.

her hand is clammy; she squeezes mine, and turns to kiss me lightly on
top of my head, as though i am the one that needs comforting.
i pretend i am, because that is the way you comfort Mami. because love does not always have be honest, because love
sometimes sacrifices truth for peace of mind.

i hear it when Mami yells and i feel it when the palm of her hand
meets my cheek. i see it when her eyes open wide and i taste
it when my tears meet my tongue. her voice is steady when
she tells me this hurts her more than it hurts me.

Mami's mother's hand was heavier, her love harder. i've traced the
scars that never quite healed on Mami's upper arms and she tells
me not to worry; Mami's love is different than her mother's.

i hear it in her tone-deaf lullabies that lull me to sleep; i feel
it when she strokes my hair. i see it clearest as my eyes
close gently when i finally drift off to sleep.

i find it in the letters in my drawers that Mami doesn't know i have; those
signed with her name and addressed to my father. i don't tell her i
have them because love can be proud; i know this because my letters
are filed away, too, signed with my name, unsent and unstamped.

when the time comes, we stand at once and our hearts jump up to our throats.
the spanish i'd held there flies out of my mouth, just in time to greet her.

hola, mamá maría, cómo está? is all i need to get out before i am smothered by thin-lipped kisses; i am enveloped by her soft, small body.

i feel guilty when my first instinct is to pull back into my mother, who smiles with tears spilling down her cheeks.

i wonder how many times Mami has looked at my
grandmother through watery eyes.

my mother's brown eyes stare back at me as my grandmother's small mouth
purses its small lips; i wonder if my reflection will mother like my mother,
or like my grandmother, or like no one before me. i cry for the children
that i may or may not bear, and i love them more than myself already.

Ángela Solis is a poet and writer born and raised in the San Francisco Bay Area. Her work delves into the Mexican-American identity, examining the fragments of self created by borders. Through her writing, she explores gender, class, and immigration, and pursues the careful labor of piecing these fragments together, in the endeavor of transcending borders. Ángela lives outside of San Francisco with her partner and their cat, Penelope. You can find her on LinkedIn.

Abuela

By Anna Marie Garcia

"In those days, you married who your parents chose for you."

Trembling under a white veil, rosary in her palm.
Young, naïve, pure.
Sepia tone image of an eighteen-year-old bride,
resembling a first communion photo.

Intertwined roots of the New Mexico Pinyon Pine,
Heaven-purgatory-limbo-hell.
Entrenched Catholic mission doctrine.
Duty-religion-family = life.

Questioning not her tiny Apache mother nor Spaniard father,
She glimpsed her betrothed.
Rebellious, and carnal, with slicked black hair and leather riding boots.
Self-Absorbed. To himself, a prize.

The arranged marriage. An attempt to tame him?

A miniature wooden rolling pin he made as a present,
for flat rounded bread off the fire.
Tortillas made daily, In-between giving birth,
her children learned English in school.

He drank up the profits from their family-run store,
when the open sign turned for the night.
Sought jobs in California with his two eldest sons,
she followed with five on the train.
The new house substandard, not like before.
Their sewage flushed into the bay.

Three daughters named Mary, five boys for the saints,
prayers for the still births that came.
Twenty-two years of diapers, baby at her breast,
A rosary at the end of the day.

From demolition wood and re-straightened nails,
they built her a home piece by piece.
Five bedrooms completed with only two still at home,
room for the grandkids to play.

They watched him, the next generation.
Milking his goats with grizzled full faced stubble,
stumbling from stashed wine bottles in the cellar.
They cringed when he hooted and waved his hat
at float maidens in the Fourth of July parade.

Her husband passed, she persevered.
After three times flunking driving school,
she learned to drive.
Got a job serving school lunches.
Virgin Mary kept watch on her dashboard.

In the massive house,
she pushed the tiny rolling pen
into tortillas for her grandchildren.

She loved him,
because that was what she was supposed to do.
Faith got her through.

(If she were here to read this, she'd pray a novena for me. I am blessed that
    I wasn't born in that era, I am blessed she gave me her strength.)

Anna Marie Garcia is a fiction writer, poet, and world traveler. Her creative inspiration draws from personal experience: dancing flamenco on a baroque castle stage, paragliding above Queenstown, welcoming sunrise atop Mt. Fuji, and trekking the dirt roads of third-world countries. Living half of her adult life outside the U.S., she now calls the Pacific Northwest home. She can be reached at AnnaMwritenow@gmail.com

My Daughter's Cracked Lips

By Carlos Garbiras

My Daughter's Cracked Lips
And my dad's barrita de
    manteca de cacao

Back when cigarettes used to be
manly bullets of tobacco —
the only thing capable
of killing cowboys.

When they didn't need to hide to aim
or pretend to be newfangled
entitled Millenium pens
in no need of flame.

Making the smoker
a mythical creature
in the pages
of a *fábula* —
a fable.

A time when they were simply called
what they were;
un pitillo,
un cigarro, un cigarrillo,
un canuto, o un canutillo.

In those times you needed fire
if your lungs
you wanted to turn
into a funeral pyre.

In those times you needed those
boxed matchsticks.
Those little jingly wooden beatboxes
bouncing to the beat of the
    smoker's strides.

Used to solve crimes
by detectives and novelists alike.
And that's where this plot begins;
in its reference
at a time when
I thought it was a crime.

Su cajita de manteca de cacao.
His little box of cacao butter.
The cacao butter box
was a quarter of a matchstick box.
He kept it religiously
in his pocket
for his lips;
his cracked lips,
his tired lips,
his sad lips;
his lips missing the cold
    of the mountains
his parents were born in.

Just like my lips.
Just like my daughters.

I used a chapstick for mine these days
pretending they are on a
    bed of spearmint.
And I keep that memo-
    ry with as much care
as he kept his mantequita de cacao.

I think about it
when I bent at my waist
and put some
on my daughter's lips.

Hers is different;
belonging to these times
in a way that balm
can only exist now.

As if this wasn't the future
and we are still
waiting on a tomorrow
more truthful.

One fully powered
by nuclear mini-combustion;
and a cap...
powder blue...
that would look best on a flying car
or on an old Plymouth.

Seeing her,
caressing her face,
listening to her
sound her love confessions,
I think of his scrawny frame.

Under the punishing sun
of our vapory equatorial streets;
walking with his thumbed bible
under his arm,
in his valiant frame
lacking stature and
making up for it with bravado
that was fractured.

The Napoleonic bravado
plaguing men like him
punching those in the nose
trying to stomp him
and even if some of them
were never foes
attempting to oppose him.

Up and down from oily
        and smoggy buses;
hustling to get food on two tables
struggling to find nourishment
that would make him whole.

The desire for meaning
playing tug of war with his soul;
the same cartoonish demons
camping on my sternum.

Toiling to make my blood pump
with lips that don't ache
and a heart
that never stops longing;

the events that ripped us apart
I ponder
and the ones that will for-
        ever clump us
as if we are an ephemeral daisy chain
of Cosmic dust and plunder.

Carlos Garbiras is an award-winning essayist and solo performer sorting out the deeply ingrained neurosis of a topsy-turvy upbringing in 90s Colombia, the immigrant experience in the San Francisco Bay area, the joys and stresses of modern relationships and the difficulties, indignities, and absurdities of the post-pandemic life. You can find his personal stories on telltalltale.com

My Mother Died on Earth Day

By Constance Hanstedt

We arrived five minutes late
to look into her dove-grey eyes
and whisper again
that she could let go.

A cloudy cool day,
yet I recalled how she worshiped
the sun, lathering with baby oil,
lying on a white cotton sheet
near our heirloom tomatoes.
And how she loved Sunday drives
down the back roads,
searching for hickory trees
and their fallen husks, then
cracking them open
for the sweet meat she'd stir
into fudge brownie batter.

I didn't cry that day,
but I heard her screaming.
You sold my house?
Put me in this lousy dump?
What would your father
think of his perfect girls now?

No, crying came later,
two thousand miles away
while centering a vase
of daisies on the kitchen table.
See them smile? she used to say.
The way their tiny suns pop
when you enter the room?

When they faded, I replaced
the daisies with pink tulips,
each bell shape
turned toward the light,
each sturdy stem unwavering.

Constance Hanstedt's poems have appeared in numerous literary journals, including *Rattle*, *The Comstock Review*, *Naugatuck River Review*, *Calyx*, and the *California Literary Review*. Her chapbook, *Treading Water*, was published by Finishing Line Press in 2022. She Writes Press published her memoir, *Don't Leave Yet, How My Mother's Alzheimer's Opened My Heart* in 2015. Find out more about her work at ConstanceHanstedt.com.

Retell Retail

By Elizabeth Googe

Dried, chocolate fingers run over fresh out of the box apparel.
-thirty minutes past closing time-
His mother's purple lacquered nails punch away,
halfway listening to me over the towering, brown shoeboxes.
"It has to be orange or don't bother to bring it out."
Miracle of miracles, she manages to glance up from a bedazzled iPhone.
"Sorry," she smiles at me and goes back to swiping, son do-
    ing cartwheels between the clothing racks.
A not so sorry at all.
A furious horned devil jumps inside me. The toddler has made him-
    self a playground out of pulling shirt after shirt off the plas-
    tic hangers. He hops in pleasure on top of his treasure trove.
I can already see the mess to be picked up when the doors are finally locked.
And scrubbed-
One gummy mouth sucks on a sales tag.
I swear there's a demon wink between his pudgy cheeks
    when he knocks over a well-dressed mannequin.
-and I'm already calculating how many items will go into the defective bin.
The customer comes first.
Must rinse and repeat.
The customer comes first.
Like Cinderella, the mom kicks up her feet.
Bruised bunions mere inches away, she waits for me to
    slip a tennis shoe onto her pointed toes.
And waits.
The customer *must* come first.
Pretending I'm on a Hawaiin resort, I grip her crusty
    arch and thrust it into the shoe bed.
It bulges, pushed to its threadbare limits. The store playlist loops for the
    ninth time as she struts. Acoustic rock thrumming into nothingness.
"Maybe a half size up?"
A single look says it's the craziest suggestion she's heard since someone-
God, hopefully anyone
-advised you probably shouldn't treat a depart-
    ment store as a nursery for a four-year-old.

"It would swallow me whole."
Briefly I long for quarantine days when I could use my Covid
    mask to hide displeasure rather than wear a fake smile
    for hours on end. I parrot my bicycle routine.
Feel the instep.
Touch the toe box.
Relay the price.
"Too bad this is so expensive. I can probably find it online for cheaper."
A hope of commission flickers into the distance,
dying like the forlorn sales section in the back corner.
She lounges on the worn-down bench, preparing herself to be de-shoed.
I black out the jean coverall hellion who has moved on to defacing a
    perfume advertisement, testers weighing down his pockets.
"Too bad there's no coupons…"
Let me get on my personal line to the CEO.
I bristle at the loud crash.
Another mannequin fatality.
"Yes, too bad." I can already hear the maniacal typ-
    ing of a google review in process.
Two stars, maybe one.
Who am I kidding?
This lady is a Yelp regular.
"Is the manager in?"
That bubblegum voice is soul poison.
"No, it's just me-"
Everyone else has gone home.
It doesn't stop her from collecting dresses and shorts on one arm.
"You don't mind, do you?"
The little terror runs circles around me.
Mommy dear is one leg into the dressing room.
No, the customer is not always right.

Elizabeth Googe is a former journalist turned run coach. She most enjoys writing fantasy and satirical poetry that pulls inspiration from her own day-to-day life. You can find out more by following her on Instagram @dungeons_and_dragonfruit where she talks books, fantasy, and her favorite ways to integrate running with reading.

DNA

By Jamie Armstrong

the language
that makes you *you*

the language
that makes me *me*

4 bases: A, G, C and T
built from 20 amino acids

repeated in varied sequences
3 billion-fold in each human cell

the language of living things
for 3.5 billion years

double helix
Jacob's ladder

twist of chromosomes
sky-rope of braided lianas

boa and anaconda
entwined through Amazonian art

what spawned this art?
who wrote the language?

leading one's life
following molecular instructions

the crossing of paths
the synchronicity of events

being on the same wavelength
being on the same page

so that I found you
in the moment you arrived

Jamie Armstrong co-founded The Live Poets Society of Boise, Idaho, active now for 27 years. His poems, which explore connections with nature and life's give-and-take, have appeared in *A Quiet Wind Speaks*, *This Gem of a Forest*, and other anthologies. Named "Club Poet" by the Mendocino Coast Cyclists, Jamie may be contacted at SteamDonkeyBard@gmail.com.

Forensic Files

By Jeff Walt

Every night I watch women die:
One hog-tied with her own halter top,
another chased, half bound
with duct tape, a mile from home, dinner
waiting on the table. At night I'm alone
with the TV screen while my lover sleeps.
The voyeurism, screams re-created in final scenes,
my dedication to catching the killer, the way I think
the show helps me walk safely through the world.
I love the cryptic tune that opens the show
and the narrator's forebodingly soothing voice.
I wonder if they could find
my cousin Bonnie who stripped
at The Cartwheel back in the Seventies. Her schtick
was twirling Blow Pops into herself
and bestowing them as gifts to the guys who circled
her stage. Only her bloody clothes
thrown into a ditch found
by a kid on his paper route.
I think most about Charmane Sabrah
who flagged a man on I-5 for help
leaving her mother behind to keep safe
the broken-down car as she drove off with a stranger
in his white Camaro, her rosary
always in her pocket for protection,
which her killer kept, hung as souvenir
from his rearview mirror. His wife happy
he'd finally found religion.

Jeff Walt's book, *Leave Smoke*, was published in 2019 by Gival Press and was awarded the 2020 Housatonic Book Award given by the Western Connecticut State University MFA Program. *Leave Smoke* was also awarded Runner-Up in Poetry in the 2020 San Francisco Book Festival annual competition honoring the best books of the spring. Jeff is Founder & Director of The Desert Rat Residency in Palm Desert, CA. JeffWalt.com

How to be a Poem in a Prose World

By Kenneth E Baker

When asked what you want for breakfast
talk about tans disks glistening with butter
waiting for a sensuous pour of distilled maple
set next to two white saucers with pools
of golden yolk waiting for a butter drenched
piece of toast to dive into the center
with two planks of meat marble
cooked two shades lighter than burnt
so they crunch an explosion of salty umami.

When you go to the grocery store
observe the class structure implied
by the placement of items on the shelves
notice the entitled as they mix
with the downtrodden
the irony that they all need to eat
as they stroll past the meat case.

When out with friends
talk in short phrases
use unexpected
pauses
to emphasize the idea
of people being like different cuts of meat
some prime steak others ground
and still
All
meat.

When asked what it is you do
tell people that you write poetry
along with other paying rent things.
Downplay your published works
your lack of published works
keep silent about how you are waiting

to be discovered by that someone who
will recognize the depth of your ideas
will put you on talk shows
maybe even write a poem for the inauguration
that you'll be read by others
the way your significant other reads
Rumi.
Then snap back to reality
enigmatically state,
Oh piffle, I've gone and done it again.

Then fall silent and smile and nod
while you duck out around the corner
to the emotion store to grab
a pack of middle school embarrassment
and some quick cook just turned 21 ennui
that you bring back and mix
into the nice glass of merlot
you are gazing deeply into.
Give a reassuring smile to your significant
other when they cast that
Are you alright? gaze
across the table.

Tomorrow pour all this onto blank white
happy to be rid of the dancing black
fragments of meaning,
frustrated because now
you have to go and find
the person they were meant for.

Kenneth E Baker has assumed the roles of landlord, triathlete, composer, handyman, father, fencer, data security specialist, life coach and brings all these experiences into his eclectic sensibility when writing poetry. He is a two-time finalist in the SFWC Writing Contest. His work has been included in *orangepeel literary magazine*, *OpenDoor Magazine* and *Storytelling Collective's Collective Verses | Volume I.*

I Want to Live in a Sarong

By Pat Obuchowski

I want to live in a Sarong.

I want to say good-bye
to buttoned shirts
that take too long to close.

Good-bye
to zippered pants
that cause me to take a deep breath
and pull my stomach in.

Good-bye
to those shoes
that never quite fit
and take me down a forced path.

Good-bye
to that two-cup apparatus
that stretches around my chest
and imprisons my two full breasts.

I want to live in a Sarong.
I want to feel my hair play
    on my back,
gallop on my shoulders,
and caress my soft throat as if
    seductively whispering,
"You are free...scream...sing...
    laugh out loud...whisper.
You are free."

I want to fully sense the breeze
flow through the thin green
    gauze I wear
and feel the bottom soak in the waves.

I want to open my legs so wide
I feel the caress of the ocean
as I let its scent in
as far as it desires.

I want to feel my breasts
rest ever so lightly on my over belly
where I am fully conscious
of the way they move
as I sway and swing my hips.

I want you in my arms to feel my
    full,
      warm,
        liquid belly where
      I have birthed
earth,
      mountains,
       oceans,
        sky.

Pat Obuchowski is a best-selling and award-winning author. She has written four nonfiction books, including *Gutsy Women Win: How to Get Gutsy and Get Going*. Although relatively new to the world of poetry writing, her poems have been published in *The Journal of Undiscovered Poets* and *Redwood Writers Club 2023 Phases* poetry anthology. Connect with her on LinkedIn.

Children's
and
Young Adult

Category Winner:
Veilweaver

By Oscar King IV

It was the day of her father's funeral, and rather than mingle with the mourners or nod through cringy commiserations, Hazel occupied herself by pilfering what materials she could from the many expensive tapestries that filled the great manor.

It was not mere silk or fine wool that Hazel stole from the long halls and ornate antechambers. The hanging artworks that covered the walls did not have any such mundane fabric: no wefts of wool strings of silk. This was Akacia, and so it was not threads of dyed cloth that she pinched, delicately pulled like big bills from a fat wallet. This was Akacia, so each tapestry in the manor's regal passageways was vapor itself: captured and spun by the magic of Veilweaving.

Cirrus clouds, and cumulonimbus right on the cusp of lightning, and even the fleeting sunrise mist that had been freshly dyed in the sun's dying red light.

Hazel concentrated, letting her Will bleed into the Veilwoven fabric. Even though the tapestry was a priceless work of art, the manor's new owners wouldn't miss it; they had plenty of money, plenty of tapestries, plenty of Veil, while she had nothing.

And besides, this whole place had once been her home. She just needed to steal enough Veil to knit one outfit; she could sell that outfit for enough money to buy more Veil, and then she could make another outfit, sell it, and on and on until she had enough money to buy her way out of Akacia, to get on a boat to Velryk or Grandia or anywhere but here. She could do it.

Though it pained her to use her art this way, what choice did she have? Akacia hadn't seen clouds in months. This was her only option.

She exhaled, closing her eyes and letting her Will fill the vaporous channels of the artwork.

With a pulse of her Veilweaving she unWove the tapestry. The entire structure convulsed, shuddered, then erupted into a flowing creature of smoke and ash and cloud particles.

Provided your Will was strong enough and your hands dexterous enough, you could shape Veil into anything. As quickly as she had unWoven the tapestry, Hazel reshaped it. She drew the vapor and the smoke into tight lines, fashioning the tapestry's Veil into inconspicuous little bundles of Veilwoven fabric, each no bigger than a finger.

Where once there had been a lovely tapestry, ten feet by ten feet, there was now nothing but bare wall.

Hazel had to move quickly; she had only made a brief appearance so far, and after all, it was her father they were here to honor.

She smirked at the irony of the thought: *Honor* was perhaps the wrong word. As was '*father*,' perhaps.

Hazel tried to look calm and collected as she moved through the twisting hallways and into the wide gardens, lush with greenery. The funeralgoers were mingling about, trading faux somber memories about the late Mr. Géraud Sauvageau, gone so soon, what a tragedy. Barely halfway to a hundred, what a tragedy. And after his wife left him so suddenly. At least the new owners of the estate were generous enough to host the funeral here. Yes, how generous.

As Hazel walked briskly through the gardens, she tried to ignore the guests' chatter.

Whatever she couldn't ignore, she gathered up and crammed deep down inside her, knotting it with a little bow so that it could never come loose.

If only this many people had shown up when her father needed them.

Hazel found herself bristling. Her scarf also seemed to shiver, like a feline suddenly perturbed. It caught up in the mild wind and began to dance around her. Or not dance, *fly*. It wasn't just a scarf that surrounded her: it was her truest masterpiece.

The billowing scarf was nearly eight feet long, but it never touched the ground. Instead, it floated about her, constantly flitting and shapeshifting just like the clouds she'd used to knit it.

Even in the dry heat of the day, the scarf provided a soothing coldness on her skin, almost like mist but without the wetness. Which was appropriate because the scarf *was* mist without wetness. It was mist, and it was clouds of a dozen varieties, and it was smoke: smoke of pine, of cedar and of hickory, and cherry, maple, mesquite, alder, and on and on.

When Hazel inhaled the scent of her scarf, she was inhaling the first breath she'd ever taken; she was inhaling the memories of her deceased brother, of her disappeared mother, and of a hundred clouds as priceless as they were beautiful.

Soon, her father would be in her scarf as well. Before the evening was over, Hazel's father would be cremated. Hazel had to catch the smoke and Veilweave it first into her scarf, and then into the Sauvageau family pattern – a massive Veilwoven arras made of every member of the Sauvageau household from back when Espiraea had first colonized Akacia's little island nation.

It was a stupid tradition. Who would ever *want* to be sewn into a giant blanket with a bunch of dead relatives? If it were her, she'd want to be borne away on a breeze. She'd want to become the mist and seafoam and the wind itself. To become *lightning*, even.

Across the gardens and three thousand feet below the massive wall, the Sloping Sea smashed against the mountain. What a power it would be to become vapor, to turn into sea mist and float out over the cliff and be lost into seafoam and thunder and the vast sea that hung above the ocean. She imagined that she could spin herself into a cloud, set herself drifting over the ocean and away from the day that awaited her, from the guests and their "I'm sorry for your losses," as though condolences were coins to be collected to buy back a father. Or, not so much of a father.

A small nucleus of well-dressed men and women talked nearby. Their voices were hushed. The guests expected her to be broken and shaken; they expected her to mourn. They did not expect her to feel free, at last, from this cursed family and the grand burden it had heaped upon her life.

Quickly, and trying to appear nonchalant, Hazel hurried away from the main clusterings of guests. Hoping that her haste wasn't obvious, Hazel drove through the gardens toward an entrance into the back half of the mansion.

She turned the familiar corners, avoiding eye contact with the servants who used to work for her. She made one turn, then another, walked through an open archway onto a long balcony with grand arches to let in the spray of the ocean and the smell of the warm summer air.

Out of pure habit, Hazel reached out one window to grab the clouds and pull them down, but there were no clouds to grab. This, to her, was the greatest indignity of all. She knew the clouds better than anyone; the least they could do was show up when she wanted.

The sea itself foamed its discontent at the bare, brutal sky. Like an azure blanket shaken to get the dust out, the ocean lashed and churned at the dead, empty air.

At last, Hazel came to the place she was searching for: another hallway, sufficiently away from the guests' prying eyes. She counted down the line of tapestries until she found the one she wanted: a shapeshifting tableau of altostratus and volcanic ash and the first fog of spring.

She exhaled slowly, grabbing the fringes of the tall fabric. Anyone could Veilweave. The art was like singing opera or playing pianoforte or learning a foreign language. It might take some practice, and natural talent and the age one started learning might help, but anyone could do it.

Certainly, some people were more skilled at Veilweaving than others. The tapestry she now held had been knit by a true master. The materials alone were worth a whole family's yearly salary, but Hazel thought the artwork itself was a waste. Veil was meant to be worn. It was meant to become you, define you as any good outfit does. Putting a material as versatile and gorgeous as Veil into some stagnant, decorative blanket like this was just... just unethical. Veil should be free, should be walked through the city streets where it could buoy up on the wind.

This rationalization made it easier for her to take hold of the fabric and, with another push of her Will, deconstruct it down to its base parts, which she promptly condensed and hid on her person.

"I won't tell anyone," said a voice behind her.

Hazel startled, turning. She knew this voice. She'd heard it a hundred times on the radio. Everyone in Akacia had.

Before her stood Magnate Nathanael Gómez himself: Akacia's nationally elected ruler and first Curranian democratic president.

Oscar King IV is a Bay Area-based English teacher and writer whose work draws from global stories of resistance, fairy tales, and finding wonder in the mundane. When he isn't working with emerging writers, he's likely solving some new riddle or reading first drafts to his two dachshunds. Discover more at OscarKingIV.com

Hatched

By Allison M. Bell

The Empty Cage

In Swumperland, no cage sits empty for long.

At least, that's how it was right up until the day the new terrarium appeared, the one with a plastic skull inside.

The Swumper brothers—Ray and Bill—knew that an empty cage would disappoint the tourists. Their hand-painted sign promised "Creatures of the Swump," not "Empty Cages of the Swump." It was true that most of their customers didn't ask about Swump Creatures—mostly they wanted a cold soda and some air conditioning—but the Swumpers suspected that if that soda came with a taste of excitement, of danger even, the visitors might stay a little longer. They might invest in an airboat ride or a paid tour of the alligator pond out back. They might post some photos, maybe even a viral video or a five-star review.

The first "taste of excitement" was plucked straight off the dock behind Swumperland: a squat pig frog. He was chosen not because he was dangerous but because he did not cost any money (though it should be noted that he was so slippery, Bill Swumper nearly fell into the pit of alligators trying to capture him). Once the frog was finally secured in a cage, Bill carried him straight to a high shelf at the back of the gift shop and hurried off to wash his hands. There the frog sat, alone and croaking to himself, earning mostly amused smiles and a few extra postcard sales.

The Swumpers needed something bigger, more dangerous, something that visitors could more easily touch. On a warm winter day, they brought in a second cage. This cage was larger than the first, and it took both of the Swumpers to heave it onto the wide shelf below the pig frog. Then, Ray disappeared through the glass doors at Swumperland's entrance. Bill stayed behind, unraveling a homemade banner that read "Swump Selfies Here" in an ugly, oozing green font. By the time Ray returned with a heavy, writhing sack, the banner hung crooked above the shelves, welcoming the python to its new home.

The snake was a wild success, a star on social media with hundreds of followers. Soon, Bill's whole day was booked up with airboat rides, and Ray's with animal tours. They were too busy to spend much time trapping more animals for their budding zoo, though Bill did scoop one red-bellied turtle out of the water on an airboat ride. It delighted the guests so much that he brought it back to Swumperland. Ray dug up a five-gallon tank from the shed and slid the turtle's new home onto the shelf beside the python.

The python, the turtle, and the frog worked their magic on the tourists all through the spring. But when summer came—the hottest on record—the python's followers were content to watch him from the cool comfort of their backyard pools.

The Swumpers began to scheme again. They needed something new, something exotic, something that could not be seen in any old Florida canal. And now, they had a little savings to spend.

An order was placed. It would take six to eight weeks to arrive.

The fourth cage appeared on the shelf between the python and the turtle.

The speculation began immediately.

The python, whose name was Ziggy, daydreamed that the cage would be home to a snake. A smaller snake, of course, maybe a coral snake or a king snake, one whose scales would not chafe against the glass as his own did. This snake, impressed by Ziggy's size and wisdom, would eagerly adopt the python as a mentor.

Ziggy did not share this daydream with anyone. In his heart, he knew it was a selfish wish. The best outcome, truly, would be if the cage sat empty forever, its intended occupant roaming the swamp freely, unaware that it had evaded capture.

The turtle, on the other hand, saw no need to keep her opinions to herself.

"I hope it's a skunk," Greta announced when the cage appeared between hers and Ziggy's. It was clear from the venom in her voice that she had a rather personal reason for this wish, but no one asked her about it.

"Gorf," croaked Slipper from above. Ziggy cringed a little as he said it. (It was a perfectly sensible response, but speaking in one syllable at a time makes it hard to be understood). Ziggy waited for Greta's sigh. It came on cue.

As days passed, then weeks, and still the Swumpers did not produce a coral snake or a skunk, each of the neighbors felt a little disappointment and a little relief. The slight stirring of excitement faded from the room. In its place came a familiar melancholy.

One night, during a fierce spat of rain, a small green lizard sought refuge in Swumperland. None of the animals noticed.

They did not hear the lizard slip quietly through the glass doors, creep past the racks of human treasures, and scamper up the back wall toward the soft red glow of the new cage. They did not see her peer down from the cage's lidless rim into a warm, dry shelter. They did not notice her curl up under the skull, lulled to sleep by the raindrops on the tin roof. And in the dawn, they did not hear the gentle words the lizard murmured before she left.

Even by the light of day, when the lizard was long gone, no one noticed what she had left behind on the mossy floor of the cage: a tiny egg.

Not Hatching

Inside the tiny egg was a tiny lizard. His name was Bernard, and he spent the next several weeks doing his very best not to hatch.

His egg was warm. It was snug. It felt safe. It was the only home he had ever known. He had no desire to leave it. And he had every reason to suspect that the outside world would be a terrible downgrade.

This impression came mostly from the ominous sounds he heard through the shell. There were croaks, deep and steady. An occasional plunk. Rustling. Bernard had no names for most of these sounds, much less any idea where they came from. He lay curled up in the darkness, ear pressed to his shell, with no way of knowing whether the creatures who made those noises cared for the taste of lizard.

The most frightening sound was the clomping. It came at regular intervals, and Bernard always felt it before he heard it. Whatever creatures made the noise were so massive that the ground shuddered as they neared. There were many clomps at one time, inspiring Bernard to imagine a whole herd of clompers or perhaps one colossal, many-limbed creature. Neither prospect made him want to leave his egg.

But eventually, not-hatching became unbearably uncomfortable. Bernard's body had grown so much that it threatened to burst out of the shell without bothering to ask permission.

And so, on his thirty-fifth day in the egg, he yielded. With one long claw, Bernard sliced open his shell, and he poked his head out into the world for the very first time.

At first, everything was blinding and blurry. He sat there, half his body still in the egg, blinking and blinking and blinking.

Then, something came into focus. It was Bernard's right foot. He tilted an eye toward it—his eyes were on either side of his head—and examined it carefully.

He had five toes, skinny but long, with bulbous tips. Bernard would have thought they were shaped like a snail's antennae, if he had ever seen a snail before. His toes were green. Bright, beautiful green.

He was mesmerized. Up until that moment, his entire life had been lived in various shades of darkness.

When he finally tore his eyes away from his toes, he saw with a pang that the soft shell was crumpling around him. He pulled himself the rest of the way out of his egg, unfurled his brand-new tail, and stretched.

This was no ordinary stretch. It was a delectable, bone-creaking stretch, the sort one can only take a few times in one's life. He tested his tail, curling it upwards, to the left, to the right. He lifted his head and felt the beginnings of his dew lap pushing out from his throat. It would be weeks still before it became a full-fledged flag, one he could display to claim his territory. But it felt good to know it was there.

The stretch, together with the fresh air warm against his wet scales, infused him with energy. It gently tickled his limbs to life, and it planted a tiny speck of curiosity in his heart. With extraordinary caution and the smallest bit of hope, Bernard set out to explore his new world.

Allison Bell is a middle-grade writer and educator based in Oakland, California. Connect with her on LinkedIn.

Lupe Throws Like a Girl

By Anita Perez Ferguson

Lupe crammed a Live Healthy frozen meal into the microwave and turned the TV on to the Women's Softball Finals. Someday she would pitch in the finals. She wondered, what would Coach Nancy say about this three-minute meal? The package stated, 'Boost your stamina and liveliness without additional fat and carbs.'

Dinner was ready, and the opening pitch was about to be delivered. Lupe climbed into Dad's beloved chair. All alone, she propped her meal on her lap. Mom was at work trying to support the family. Lupe had no other friend except Penny, who was at her family's lake house. David, Lupe's brother, was cruising in Dad's classic Chevy.

The meal was average, nowhere as delicious as Mom's Chili Colorado. Dinner was bland without the fat and carbohydrates or enchiladas, tortillas, and beans. Lupe reminisced about the past when it was her responsibility to clear the table while Mom cooked. David's mitt, nicknamed Roberto, always landed on the dinner table.

"*Afuera*, outdoors, David!" Mama constantly reminded David to keep his baseball mitt out of the dining room.

The initial inning of the softball finals was lackluster. The second-hand TV looked fuzzy. Lupe reminisced about the happy bygone days, which were only a year ago. David was home. He took time to have a catch with her. Mom was not forced to work all the time, and Papa was alive. She unlaced her shoes, still warm from the afternoon's softball practice, and tossed them in the corner. Mom's words echoed in Lupe's head, urging her to make them proud. Her understanding of pride was based on both spotless white shoes and winning games.

Lupe's softball cleats dropped, stirring up a cloud of dust. They rested there, standing out from Mom's tidy house, small but clean. Lupe never asked Penny to visit her home, no matter how spotless it was. When the college recruiter requested to speak with Mom, Lupe told her that all the meetings occurred at the school campus. She was convinced that every single person on the school team lived like Penny, on the hill, two cars, with college savings. After all, they were all tall, slim, and blond.

Lisa Fernandez, Lupe's role model, appeared in the game on TV. She pitched for UCLA. Lupe struggled to make out the details on the tiny TV screen. She analyzed Lisa's stance on the mound and her delivery. *There is nothing I wouldn't do to be part of a college team like her. How am I going to make anyone feel proud of me, living alone in this cramped house, having a frozen dinner every night while my Mom is away at work? David, my dropout brother, pretends to be the bigshot. I have to make it through graduation.*

The next Monday, with images of Lisa Fernandez still in her mind, Lupe tugged at her laces, smudged with dirt from the infield. Mom would be irate. The shoes cost too much to be dirty. That was the way she preferred them. It was the way the shoes of the rest of the girls appeared.

"You put on a great show for that recruiter today. You might as well have had a big sign on your jersey saying, I'm a pitcher!" Penny teased Lupe.

"You're nuts. Think about it, in one month, we'll be at the training camp, and then we can show off." They worked as a team, the pitcher and the catcher. Penny and Lupe almost had softball scholarships guaranteed. Lupe folded her uniform. She would throw it in the wash tonight after she cleaned up the kitchen. Something was sticking out of the back pocket. Lupe removed a note, her mother's constant reminder. Make us feel proud, in Spanish, '*haznos sentir orgullosos.*'

"Yeah, camp, cool," Penny nodded. The swinging doors of the girls' locker room pushed inward, and a nerdy freshman strode in with her chin jutting out as she gawked at the half-naked players. "What are you doing here?" Feet astride, hands on her hips, Penny blocked the passage for the girl. Sometimes she could be mean.

"Who are you, the panty police? Put some clothes on and let the kid in." Lupe worked to elicit laughter from Penny.

"I'm looking for Lupe Lopez and Penny Williams. The freshman declared she had a note from Ms. Granger in the Counseling Office.

"Oh, Luuu-pe, Pen-nee!" The rest of the players taunted. "Are you in trouble?"

Lupe never believed her teammates liked her. She was at least two inches shorter than all of them and ten pounds heavier. Everyone on the team had a nickname, and hers was Squatty Body. The only place she detected approval was when she was on the mound, pitching her fastball past all the hitters.

"Give me that note." Lupe knew high school was one problem after another. Her family was counting on her to be the first to receive a diploma.

As a freshman, Lupe was placed in classes with kids who had difficulty reading. She had typing, and shop, and cooking. At least those classes taught her something practical. Her grades were satisfactory, so in her sophomore year, she was assigned to more difficult classes. Then she felt like she could not comprehend the written word. Her homework was unreal, and she had to buy a bunch of extra books that Mom could not afford. Dad was in and out of the hospital that year. Lupe used the worn-out ratty library books underlined by other poor kids. That summer, Dad died of a heart attack.

Lupe tried out for the softball team on a dare from her brother. She loved the sport. When she joined the team, she did not know anyone. Most of the other girls were debutant types who wore designer jeans. Penny and Lupe dreamed of getting admitted to the university to play sports after graduation. They joked about being salt and pepper, the tall girl with pale skin and the short dark girl.

Lupe read the counselor's note. 'Girls, come to my office as soon as possible. I depart the campus at 5:35.'

"Penny, we gotta go. Come on." The two girls raced out of the locker room and toward the Counselor's office.

"What's this all about?" Penny had no trouble keeping pace with Lupe, thanks to her long legs. Her ponytail swished behind her.

"I have no idea what this is about. It's always something. I can't wait to graduate and escape from here." *What was the problem? Was her brother in an accident?* At 5:23, the girls knocked on Ms. Granger's door.

"Close call, girls," the counselor opened the door, prepared to leave her office, "you are both in big trouble."

"Both of us?" They spoke in unison.

"Yes, my records reveal that neither one of you completed your sixty hours of community service required for graduation."

"What? Don't sports count? We don't have time for anything else when we have practice every day. We just now left the field." Lupe had a bad feeling about this.

"Sports are good, and if you were coaching little kids, that could count. But just being on the team, I'm afraid not. You are fortunate I received a request for volunteers today. It will be ten hours a week for the last six weeks before graduation."

"But we have a practice. We can't manage this." Lupe and Penny groaned in disbelief.

"Volunteer service is mandatory before graduation. The law requires it. It's Monday, Wednesday, and Friday, 5:45 to 7:45, after practice, just down the street at Villa Santa Barbara."

"What's that?" Penny said.

"The retirement home — never!" Lupe knew the place all too well. Her mother washed the retirees' laundry on the midnight shift.

"Ugh!" Penny uttered.

"You receive a complimentary meal. Spend one hour eating with the residents and another hour visiting after dinner. It's easy."

"You must be joking." Lupe was mortified. It was tough enough to fulfill the hours, but at the same place Mama handled the dirty laundry? That was why she aspired to get her diploma, to gain something better with her life.

"What is on their menu?" Penny said.

"They have normal food, Penny. And they are waiting for you." The counselor shooed them away. "Go introduce yourselves tonight. Now get going."

Anita Perez Ferguson is the award-winning historical fiction author of the Mission Bells Trilogy. *Lupe Throws Like A Girl* is the first book in her contemporary fiction series for teens. Diverse Voices – Bravo! Featuring Latinx authors at AnitaPerezFerguson. com & AnitaPerezFerguson.substack.com.

Burning Daylight

By Ayushi Thakkar

1: Bria

There's that moment when someone dies, isn't there? That precise moment when their eyes transition from life to absence. When their gaze shifts from fixating on something to staring into absolute emptiness. Most people never see when that happens to someone. Most people have never witnessed death.

Bria had. Or rather, she was always meant to.

She'd known that her entire life. But the first time it had become real, really *real,* was when she was twelve. That was when the Ringleader had first placed a knife into Bria's hand and explained how to hold it.

That was the first time she had thought, *'I'm going to kill someone.'*

Six years later, Bria still thought that. But it wasn't *'I'm going to kill someone'* anymore.

Now, it was *'I'm going to kill someone who has wronged me.'*

Was that any better?

To some people, maybe not. For Bria, it made a vital difference.

It was what was running through her head as she threw knives held along her belt at the targets hung along the walls of the abandoned office the Retaliators used for their operations. With exceptional precision, she struck each one, nailing the red circle positioned right at the center of the bullseye.

She hit the final target with a *thunk* as the knife sank into the wood.

After, Bria expected to hear silence as she normally did. Instead, the door flung open. An inkling of fear flashed through her as she imagined who it could be..

A civilian?

A police officer?

Worse?

However, the feeling vanished when Bria matched the footsteps with a person in her memory.

Long-short-long-short.

That walk belonged to someone who had a permanent limp. That walk belonged to the Ringleader. Bria turned around and smiled.

"Hi Dad," she said.

"Hello Bria," he responded, glancing at the knife in the last target. "It needs to be deeper."

A hint of irritation flickered inside her. It was true; it could be deeper. It was also at an angle. But she didn't need him to point it out.

He limped over to the target and pulled out the knife. Little splinters of wood rained from the hole in the weapon's wake.

The Ringleader didn't look like a Ringleader. Scalp shone through his cropped blonde hair. Piercing blue eyes bulged out of his skull and his cheeks were a rosy pink. The features fit into a face sort of shaped like a potato.

Between him and Bria, the only similarity seemed to be the shape of their nose. And, if you counted it, perhaps the blonde highlights running through her hair could be a giveaway. But those didn't get there through genetics.

Luckily, Bria didn't look much like what was lost just a few weeks after her brother was born. She liked that. Maybe that meant she had the opportunity to be her own person.

The Ringleader held out the knife to her and ordered, "Try again,"

Begrudgingly, Bria took the knife and threw it again. It landed in the middle of the target again, but now, the blade was deeper than before and perfectly parallel.

Her father didn't praise her. Or applaud. He simply nodded sharply. He didn't linger on it either. The Ringleader glanced at his watch and said, "It's almost time."

Bria pursed her lips and followed him out of the room. They walked down a hall and stopped at the wall. Then the Ringleader bent down and placed a hand on the floor, fingers spread out, and he twisted his hand to the right. Bria pushed herself against the wall as a trapdoor opened.

Bria crept through first, landing on her feet in the underground room. The Ringleader jumped in after her.

It wasn't a huge room. There was a table in the middle covered in photos and papers. There was no electricity, just melted candles sitting on the edges of the floor. Bria pulled out a matchbox from her pocket and went around and lit each, little fires coming to life inside each one of them. After, she put away the matchbox, picked up the last candle, and held it in her hands. The Ringleader walked to the table and looked over it, picking up certain papers and setting them away from the others.

Victims.

But not really. They wronged them. They are it. This wasn't murder. It was revenge. Retaliating against the offenders.

A few minutes later, the trapdoor opened. Bria wasn't afraid this time. She knew who was coming. Slowly but surely, more and more people were filing into the room, picking up a candle and holding it. Some had cameras around their necks, while others had pocket knives. Either way, they were an essential part of the Retaliators. Finally, all the candles were lifted from the floor, meaning everyone was there.

Wait. No.

A single forsaken candle lay in the corner. Everyone was here but one.

She had a sneaking suspicion of who it was.

Bria looked around the room again. The faces of the men, women, and people in the hidden hideout were illuminated by the light in their hands, but the one Bria was looking for wasn't among them. Oh no. He wasn't here.

"He's late," called out a woman in the front of the room named Jessica. "Again."

The Ringleader made a quiet *tsk* noise. "Of course, he is. He is *always* late."

Bria ground her teeth together but kept her face neutral. *Maybe it's not his fault. Have you ever considered that, Father?*

She knew he did. She also knew that he was choosing to ignore it. Nobody in the Retaliators really cared about his perspective. All they needed was an excuse to blame him, and they almost always found one.

But he wasn't the one who had done anything. Not unless you counted him being born a crime.

She knew it wasn't his fault. She knew there was probably some external barrier stopping him from arriving on time. She knew she'd hear all about it later.

Bria rolled her eyes in disappointment at the group, who were quietly murmuring to each other. Hopefully, it would look like she was rolling her eyes at *him*.

After a few more minutes of waiting, the Ringleader sighed and declared, "We're starting. He'll have to catch up on whatever he misses. It's only *his* fault he is late."

2: Adri

Adri was going to get murdered.

Not *really*, of course. Verbally. But it would still be bad. The Retaliators didn't care about *why* he was late; they just cared that he *was*.

He worked a double shift and was now rushing back home to pick up his camera. He couldn't control that the coffee shop was on the other side of town from his apartment. Or the fact that the bus he needed was late because of traffic. Nobody cared that there were things that were out of his control. They just cared that he couldn't control them. There was a difference.

Adri was in such a panic that it took him three tries to turn his key in the correct direction to open the door to his apartment. It wasn't a huge place. One bedroom, one bathroom, and the yellow paint was peeling off the corners of the walls. There wasn't a couch, but rather a single chair that was unfortunately under-stuffed. The plastic table was surrounded by two folding chairs. Still, it was the only place he could afford, so he made it work.

His camera was sitting on the table. He picked it up and placed it around his neck. It was probably the nicest thing he owned, though the Nikon D850 hadn't been in his possession for long. For a long time, he had been using a camera he bought at Goodwill, but that wasn't a good camera; the resolution was horrible, and he couldn't take videos. The Ringleader was dissatisfied with his work and had given him a new camera. Adri had been ecstatic to receive it, but the dark look in the Ringleader's eyes at the time left a dark shadow over the memory.

Adri grabbed his keys and locked the door to his apartment

Luckily, the walk to the Mares' office building wasn't long. Even shorter because he ran. Adri wasn't exactly sure what the company did, but when all workers left after finishing their nine-to-five shift for the day, it was used for meetings for the gang that haunted the streets of New Brook, Virginia: The Retaliators.

Ayushi Thakkar, age 14, is a freshman in high school. When she emerges from piles of homework, she enjoys reading mystery and fantasy with jarring twists and mythical elements. She enjoys singing for her school chorus, Bollywood/indo-contemporary dance, and writing, of course. She also loves making playlists for her favorite fictional characters, listening to Taylor Swift, and annoying her little sister.

Dancing Ants

By Carlos Garbiras & Justine Rege

Out into the world
and ready to explore,
a mother and her daughter
venture past their front door.

They came to a trail,
as the path became wider,
they spotted lots of flowers,
a dragonfly, and a spider.

Just ahead on the trail
was a big dirt dome,
with a long line of ants
coming back to their home.

Mom pointed out how
they marched perfectly in line,
working hard to return
to their families in time.

The daughter watched for a bit
and she saw something change.
They broke their line into groups;
that can't be! It seems strange!

With a great big smile,
...and twirl...and a prance,
she sang loudly as she could
"Those there are dancing ants!"

Mom pulled out a magnifying glass
so they could really see!
The whole scene was an amazing show
with costumes, music, and glee!

Entering center stage
is a fancy ant in a top hat.
Dancers take their places
and introductions start just like that.

First up is Amy and Bob.
Breaking, locking, and popping.
They know how to hip-hop;
they do it without stopping.

Joette steps in.
She dances ballet.
She simply loves the spotlight
as she takes her curtsy in plié.

Joette' daughters are next.
They're called Isadora and Bjorn;
they refuse all instruction
and rebel against form.

They don't like ballet
they are free as wild canaries,
they move with the wind
that's why they chose contemporary.

Emilio and Laura
begin a tropical Tango,
for no other reason
than they really like Mango.

Then five tapping friends,
Elsa, Emma, Edna, Etta,
　　and Gertrude,
make little clicks and clacks
with the toes and heels of their shoes.

They create their own music,
moving together on the beat.
What a special and unique sound,
the drumming of 30 tiny feet!

Maria and Hector love to salsa;
this beat it is not for eating
it's for dancing and spinning
and shouting and singing.

Willie and Lindy do-
    ing the Charleston;
ankle twists, bent knees and kicks,
what a rush and a surprise,
when they finished with a lift!

Marla and Harlem
dancing snazzy jazz;
with white gloves on their hands,
they move with such pizzazz.

They like to improvise
and to get the audience involved,
creating conversation between
movement, instruments, and all.

The ant with the top hat
returned to center stage,
"There you have it, my friends,
Dancing Ants are all the rage!"

Next time you pass by
something appearing com-
    mon or plain,
look a little closer and perhaps...
you'll see a dance party again!

As for the mom and her daughter,
they'll have this memory together.
Curiosity and imagination;
the best adventure ever!

Carlos Garbiras is an award-winning essayist and solo performer sorting out the deeply ingrained neurosis of a topsy-turvy upbringing in 90s Colombia, the immigrant experience in the San Francisco Bay area, the joys and stresses of modern relationships and the difficulties, indignities, and absurdities of the post-pandemic life. You can find his personal stories on telltalltale.com

Justine Rege and her daughter were on a walk when they ran into an anthill. Their daughter looked at the ants in it and shouted, "They look like dancing ants." After that, Carlos and Justine decided to write this story.

Jubilee Watson and the Mystery of the Peanut Butter Key

By Derek Wheeless

"You are the one who stole the key." I raised one eyebrow and leveled my eyes on the thief.

The room had gone still as if the very air had been sucked from it, and I sensed everyone staring at me and the culprit. They had questions, no doubt.

"Are you sure?" Aunt Artica stood beside me, her hand resting on my shoulder. "How do you know?"

"How do I know?" I looked up at our school counselor and smiled. "Because I am Jubilee Watson. I solve crime with my mind. And I am the greatest kid detective ever."

The morning had started like any other.

Trace crumpling Newsha's homework. A lesson with our school counselor Miss Doss and her therapy dog Mister Rigby. And a chapter quiz on *The Westing Game*. Only Dice made a perfect score.

[Art note: Dog is licking Newsha's fingers.]

"I missed problem two?" Newsha whined. She hated missing even one question.

Mrs. Middleton showed her the answer key.

[Art note: The teacher has made a mistake on number two on her answer key and corrected it.]

Newsha pouted. Jac read a book. Mateo and Dice high-fived. Trace drew on the back of his quiz.

Another routine day at Edgar Allan Poe Elementary.

Until lunch, when Dice waved me over to the peanut-free table.

"I hear you solve mysteries, Jubilee."

I slipped him my card. "I solve crime with my mind. What's on *your* mind?"

[Art note: Cards say "Invisible Think Detective Agency. We solve crimes with our minds."]

"This morning, I switched cubbies with Trace to be next to Mateo. Then, Mrs. Middleton found her answer key in my new cubby. It was stolen during recess yesterday. She has a meeting with my parents after school. I didn't steal it. Honest. Will you take my case?"

I looked around. Trace was smearing peanut butter in Newsha's hair. Mateo was frowning at his lunch. Jac was reading.

And the smell of hot rolls was making me hungry.

"I'll take it," I said. "Crime doesn't pay, but it'll cost *you* two dollars a day."

Dice agreed, and I got right to sleuthing on the playground.

I needed some suspects, and the recess restroom list was the first stop in my investigation.

[Art note: List shows when kids left the playground and went to the classroom restroom. "Sign to go in. Sign when you come out. One student at a time, please." Dice: 12:03 – 12:06, Mateo: 12:09 – 12:14, Trace: 12:16 – 12:20, Newsha: 12:21 – 12:21, Jac: 12:21 – 12:25.]

Then it was time for suspect interviews.

I found Jac shooting baskets on the court. I played it coy. "Notice anything suspicious yesterday?"

Jac shrugged. "The cafeteria spaghetti didn't taste like sweaty socks for once?"

I found Newsha by the slide, still upset about her quiz. "Mrs. Middleton's answer key must be wrong!"

I found the boys playing football. Trace clammed up but not Mateo. He was scowling.

"This morning, somebody tore apart the PB&J I had in my cubby!"

Coming in from recess, I discovered the counselor changing her bulletin board.

"Got time for a question, Miss Doss?" I asked.

She smiled. "Does Nancy Drew like a clue?"

I handed her a sticky piece of tape. "How was Mr. Rigby after your lesson today?"

"Thirsty!" She let out a loud whistle. "Guzzled water like it was from a firehose."

Back in the classroom, I tried to focus on spelling, but my mind was on the mystery.

And Dice's parent meeting was ticking closer by the minute!

Then it hit me.

Because this complete picture book text was under 1500 words, it was entered into the contest in its entirety. But as this anthology is meant to be a sampler of work by emerging authors, we're cutting it short to protect the author's future publishing plans. If you like reading mysteries with the kids in your life, keep an eye on his website for future publication dates!

Derek Wheeless lives in Frisco, Texas, and has published several mystery short stories for adults as well as the young adult novel *We Planned a Murder*. Discover more about him and his work at DerekDWheeless.com

Wilder

By Jocelyn Forest Haynes

"Did you vote for him too?"

"What do you think?"

"Of course you did. You do everything for him."

"He's family."

"Hmph. Yeah, well, it's kind of ironic. The family who brings you in after losing your parents in a forest fire caused by humans is the same one rumored to be on their side."

"Keyword: rumored. And anyway, even if it were true, a single friendship hardly constitutes the claim of being on 'their side.' Things aren't always so black and white."

"It's Orphic law: expose yourself to no human."

"The Orphic pledge only says to be invisible. It's open for interpretation."

"I can't believe you are defending them."

"I'm not. You know I despise humans. Rather, I pity them for being so ignorant. Just speaking the truth. My Aunt Koko raised me from the time I was a baby and was the best mom any girl could ask for. Don't try to jade my memory of her just because you can't check your ego."

"I just can't believe he got voted leader over ME. I beat him in just about everything. The sling dart accuracy round-"

"You shattered his dart with yours. It was a good shot. But he still hit the bullseye."

"The tree vaulting round. By TWO trunks."

"Distance isn't the only thing that makes you good."

"And who even cares about a turkey call anyway? It's a dumb round."

"We have to eat."

"Don't even get me started on the team obstacle course. Totally unfair. Everyone was against me."

"Is that what you really think? Your team 'Rattlers' (edgy name, by the way), loses, and you throw a fit, claiming that you had the weaker group. The elders were generous doing something that had never been done before by letting you guys run the course again. It was the SAME teams. Only you got to lead the previous winners: 'Team Red Tail.' Except wait, you lost again. I think that's pretty reflective of the difference between your leadership skills and his, don't you?"

He sighed. "My father is never going to respect me now. I doubt there's anything I can do…"

"Yeah, well, don't do anything stupid. It's a lot of pressure, I'm sure- your family being so proud of its ancestors for orchestrating The Band of anti-human Orphics responsible for sabotaging the invention of the lightbulb. That was over two hundred years ago. The world sure would be a lot different place by now."

"One day, I'll join The Band."

"They were outlawed. They don't exist anymore."

"Sure they do. People talk. And if not, maybe I'll start my own."

"We're not trying to be at war."

"We're not? It's not enough to just go around cleaning up human messes in secret. INVISIBLY. Someone's got to act."

"Now you're just ranting."

He grit his teeth. "I'm bigger than him. Stronger than him. Better than him. And now I have to go out on my once-in-a-lifetime Moon Retreat- "

"OUR once-in-a-lifetime Moon Retreat."

"-with HIM being leader over ME."

"That's right. There are fourteen of us this year."

"So many eleven-year-olds…"

"Who all turn twelve this year, too. Don't forget that I'm one of them. It makes no difference. We'll travel to Little Orphica, build our mawgiws and set up our village, play lots of sky ball, hunt some turkey… It's just surviving. But, you know, without any parents or elders. No big deal. We can do that."

She paused, then added, "The moon cycle will take 29 days. You can check your ego for 29 days, can't you?"

He didn't respond.

"And when we return, we'll be accepted back into our tribe as 'equally contributing members of society.' Like grownups. We'll be all grown up."

Jocelyn Forest Haynes is a successful strength and mobility specialist with a creative soul who pulled the plug on her regular work to write the stories that have been burning inside her. Inspired by her two children, the magical forested mountains in which she lives, and gratitude for, against all odds, getting to be born and live a life, she writes middle-grade science fantasy exploring our rapidly changing world and our ever-expanding universe. You can find her on Instagram @jocelynforest

Judy & Fern

By Kiki Murphy

Judy's side:

Fern is coming over today. My mom said I'll like her, but I don't know her. What if she breaks my toys? What if she steals them? What if she's secretly a zombie and tries to eat me??? Or worse, what if she's like my little brother- gross and annoying?!

Ding Dong

Oh no, NO, SHE'S HERE!!! What do I do?!

Ok, don't panic. Deep breath in, deep breath out. I learned that from my mom.

Ah ha! I know… I need to stop her from coming inside.

"MOM, DON'T ANSWER THAT DOOR IT'S ZOMBIES I SAW THEM FROM MY WINDOW!"

"Oh Judy, don't be silly, it's just our guests! Fern is here."

Drats, that didn't work. Plan B.

SLAM (Judy slams her bedroom door shut. Signs on her door say keep out with X through zombie drawings and other various monsters)

I don't have time to waste. I'll barricade my door and tell them it's stuck. (Judy throws stuffed animals in front of her door)

Knock knock knock

"Judy? Honey, Fern is here. Can you open the door?"

"NO, I can't! Did you feel that earthquake? All my stuff just fell in front of my door! It's going to take me hours to dig myself out of here…"

(Judy's mom opens the door, sliding plushies out of the way while Judy grabs her bottle of "Zombie No More" spray bottle)

I'm zombie bait…

"Judy, meet Fern."

Are those tears in Fern's eyes? She looks scared. Why would *she* be scared?

"Oh, um, hi, Fern"

"Hi"

Fern's side:

I'm going over to Judy's house today. My mom said I'll like her, but I've never met her before. What if she's mean and won't share her toys? What if she has really boring toys?? What if she secretly has a zombie pet she keeps in her closet and feeds it people she doesn't like??? Or worse, what if she's like my older brother- gross and annoying?!

Ding Dong

I have a bad feeling about this. I don't want to go in there.

Did someone just yell something about zombies?!

I KNEW IT!!! Why isn't my mom running back to the car? What do I do??

Ok, don't panic. Deep breath in, deep breath out. My mom taught me that.

Mom must not have heard it. I just need to tell her calmly. Stay calm.

"MOM, WE CAN'T GO IN THERE I JUST HEARD THEM SAY THEY ARE GOING TO FEED US TO THEIR ZOMBIE!!!"

"Oh Fern, don't be silly. We've talked about this. People don't keep zombies as pets."

She doesn't believe me. I'm doomed.

SLAM

What was that? She must have heard me, and now she's hiding her zombie in her room.

Knock knock knock (On Judy's door)

No, no, no, nO NOOOOO, PLEEEEEEEEEEEASE! don't make me go in there!

"Awe, sweetie, it's okay. Sometimes meeting a new person can be a little scary. I think you two will have a lot of fun together. It could be fun if you give it a chance."

(Judy's mom opens Judy's door)

I'm zombie bait...

"Judy, meet Fern"

Are those tears in Judy's eyes? She looks scared. Why would she be scared?

"Oh, um, hi, Fern"

"Hi"

Judy & Fern story continued together:

"We'll be in the kitchen if you need anything. Judy, you should show Fern your dolls. Have fun girls!"

(Judy and Fern stare at each other)

(Judy sprays Fern with her "Zombie No More" spray bottle)

(Fern looks shocked)

"Why did you do that?!"

"I had to be sure you weren't a zombie. See, no zombie's allowed in my room." (Judy points to the signs on her door)

"What does it do?"

"It's a magic potion that poofs away zombies into thin air!"

"That's so cool! I need one, where did you get it??"

"My mom got it from the store. Your mom could get one too. I think my brother is turning into a zombie. He makes weird noises, and he bites. Wanna help me check?"

"Yeah! Maybe we should wear armor, though."

"Great idea!"

Kiki Murphy grew up in the Chicagoland area and recently moved to the Bay area in California with her husband and three kids. Before becoming a writer, she was a music teacher and nanny for 15 years, although she did start writing at an early age, winning a few national awards for her writing in grade school and high school. Now, as a professional freelance writer and artist, she enjoys exploring different genres and found a passion for children's literature. As an advocate for early childhood literacy, she hopes to write books that help grow and inspire a child's love for reading.

The Wasteland Crew: Knives of Kaine

By Lucinda J. Sweazey

PROLOGUE

The Year CCXXII – The South Coast of Eiland

The first eyes that saw it were in a farming outpost in the south. The children called out first, pausing their chases through neat rows of corn, asking their parents who had lit the large fire. The farmers stopped their raking to study the billowing smoke covering the horizon.

Only when the smoke hit the crops did they begin to run.

Days later, a lone child on horseback plodded into the port city of Arliander, the shawl from her dead mother drooping around her shoulders. She babbled about a fire without flame, its smoke eating her village and her family alive. The town's Premier, struck with pity at the mad girl's tales, promised they would send a scout in the morning.

The scout never left.

Screams woke the Premier and his family that same night. The southern horizon churned, black smoke crawling into town. This time a few riders escaped. But the girl, her mother's shawl draped over her body as a coffin, remained on the cobblestone.

On the smoke rolled.

Somewhere in between the fields in the south and the capital city of Centerstone it was given a name. Whispered on the backs of the few who escaped.

Ether.

CHAPTER ONE

The Year CCCV — Centerstone, The Final City of Eiland

Mor Kaine reasoned that seventeen was a respectable age to die.

She stared at the endless horizon of black smoke and the wall of crackling energy that held it back.

She didn't look down at the Tower beneath her. She didn't look over its edge at the half-dead forest scattered around it. She didn't look behind at the dim lights of the city that slept miles away.

She stared and stared at the wall of magic that stretched across the sky.

A lone man in white stood at the edge of the Tower's platform, a speck of light against a horizon of black. His arms were outstretched, hands splayed taut as if gripping the very air itself and shoving it forward. Magic poured out from him, a crackling wave that pushed against the night. The wave streamed out to either side, flowing from him as if he was force given life.

"Should have eaten a better breakfast," Mor muttered.

A snort and then silence. The figure huddled beside her waited a beat before answering.

"Do I want to ask why?"

The voice was sharp, colder than the air, but the vowels dragged similar to Mor's, the accent of the slums peaking through the words. Mor shrugged, staring at the horizon of crackling black. "Beans and porridge from the Hammer is a terrible meal to die on."

Silence.

Mor grinned and peaked over her shoulder. The darkness hid the face that was a mirror of her own, but Mor didn't need to see her face to know that her sister was scowling. Janika was always scowling.

"How is it that, no matter where we find ourselves, you are always thinking about food?"

A smile quirked across her lips, the movement tingling on a face half numb from the wind.

"A better question is, how are you not?"

The two sisters sat with their knees hugged to their chest, beneath them, stone wrapped in iron vibrated. Wind filled with the acrid taste of magic snapped at her ragged clothes. The hair on her arms stood straight from the electricity that charged the air, crackles, and pops, making her flinch half a dozen times each minute.

Mor peered again into the distance. The Anchor was a good half mile away, but she spotted it easily. The spike of iron mirrored the Tower's height, soaring above the forest beneath it as if the gods themselves had driven a spike into the ground. The Anchor glowed red hot, a slash of fire that cut the darkness. Where magic hit the Anchor, metal heated and shot the crackling energy back to the Tower and the man who stood at its center.

To the east, a second Anchor glowed. The result was a curtain of magic that stretched over a mile in diameter and a quarter as high.

A wall that held back the night.

"Water."

The order was a rasp. The man didn't even turn, wind whipping his white shirt and pants as if the uniform was a flag and the man only a pole to hold the clothes against the night.

Both Mor and Janika started, but Mor snatched the leather flask first.

She rose to a crouch and scuttled forward, a poor attempt to make herself a smaller target against the wind.

The closer she drew to the man, the more her hair stood on edge. Mor didn't know what set her more on edge — the magic that crackled inches from her or what and whom she was approaching.

A Guardian.

The man could have been chiseled from the very stone he stood. Everything about him was severe, from the cold set of his mouth to the exacting cut of his clothes, to the hair pulled tight in a knot at the base of his head. Judging from the grey slicing through that hair, Mor guessed the Guardian to be past fifty. Old for the position.

He snatched the flask from her without a word. As she waited, Mor told herself not to look down or out.

She did both.

Blood drained from her face at the sheer drop and the crackling mass of magic that loomed less than an arm's length before her. Sparks flew from the wall, landing on Mor's arms in fiery dots.

Despite the burn, her skin did not blacken.

Mor didn't have to look this time to know; the half dozen other trips up to the edge had shown her the magic didn't leave its mark on her skin.

Mor glanced nervously at the eastern sky and the wall of magic that covered it.

In the time it took the Guardian to swallow a handful of gulps, the curtain to the east faded, shifting from an endless black to a dark grey.

The Guardian tossed the flask to Mor with a curse and lifted his arm yet again. Magic poured once more from him and fortified the east flank.

Mor crouched and took a scuttling step back from the Tower's edge.

"Your kind shouldn't be near the Wall."

The Guardian's sharp words froze Mor half a pace away. Her gaze darted to her wrist, and the brand seared there. Mor opened her mouth, irritation spiking.

A throat cleared.

Mor's gaze snapped to where her sister crouched across the platform. Janika shook her head. Once. Sharply.

Swallowing a thousand retorts that would land her with fines they couldn't afford, if not worse, Mor continued her half shuffle, half crawl back to her sister. She landed in a huff, and the two sat in silence for long moments.

"I wasn't going to say anything."

"Sure you weren't."

Mor rolled her eyes, and without looking, she knew her sister did the same. The two sat in a fresh set of strained silence. Mor started when a hand settled on her wrist. Janika gave a light squeeze, her hand, scratchy with calluses from the factory, scraping against the brand that covered half of Mor's arm.

"He's letting us both be up here," Janika reminded, her soft words snatched by the wind and gone before they could reach the Guardian.

Mor huffed. "Who wouldn't want two for the price of one?"

"When it comes to you?" Janika said wryly, "Usually no one."

Mor paused. "That's offensive. I'm offended."

"No, you're not."

Mor contemplated, then jerked her chin over her shoulder to what rested behind them. "With two of us, we'll be twice as fast to get to that."

Both sisters dragged their eyes from the wall of magic to the lone item built onto the Tower's crest. A bell dominated the back center of the tower, its thick iron slope scratched with age and rust. Standing, Mor barely reached the brim, which, given her height, was saying something about the item's size. The bell soared above them both, a strange sight in a wasteland otherwise barren but for the stone Tower. And a Tower barren but for the bell. A chain linked the iron ball at the bell's center out to a hook where Janika and Mor sat.

Janika's face was still hidden in the deep night, but her voice sobered. "I don't want to find out."

Mor grimaced, arms swinging back around her knees and pulling them to her chest. She went back to staring at the wall of magic, the rippling black somehow an easier thing to watch than the bell lilting behind them.

There was only one reason the bell would ring. And Janika was right; they certainly didn't want to be the ones to ring it.

Anyone who did was dead moments later.

"I really should have had a different breakfast," Mor muttered.

Lucinda Sweazey lives in New York City, works in finance, and spends her nights writing about magic, mayhem, and villains as protagonists. She is currently working on *The Wasteland Crew*, a Young Adult Fantasy Fiction duology; this is an excerpt from the project's first book, *Knives of Kaine*. Beginning in Spring 2024, she will be seeking representation and can be reached at inquires@lucindasweazey.com.

Hiram's Heaven

By Vicki Montet

Beyond the woods, there's a place called Hiram's Heaven. Hiram was an old farmer who wore overalls and beat-up boots. Everybody talked about him like he was still around. I never met Hiram. The first time I heard about him was when Billy took me to Hiram's Heaven, to the wide-open fields where we could run until we couldn't run anymore.

It was a long walk down an old muddy dirt road to get there. It hadn't rained lately, so my new high-top tennis shoes should be okay. Mom warned me about getting dirty. I don't know why she always thought it important to tell us to stay clean.

We were kids. Kids get dirty.

Billy and I stood at the end of the dirt road. We weren't sure who owned these fields since we never met Hiram. We heard that sometimes people were out here with guns, but we didn't see anybody with guns.

"Billy, is it safe for us to just be walking around in somebody's fields? Wouldn't that be trespassing or something?" These were important questions before we started the last leg to Hiram's Heaven. "I heard some older boys came out here and got shot at Billy." Billy didn't seem to be listening much to me. He had his pocket-size binoculars out and was zoomed in on something down the road. "Shhhh Sally. Be quiet for a second. I see something."

"See something? Like what? You're scaring me." I scooted over behind him. "Billy, is somebody going to shoot at us?" He dropped the binoculars to his chest and looked at me like I was some kind of idiot.

"No, Sally, there ain't no one down this road that's going to shoot at us, so come on, let's get moving." He pulled on my shirt to bring me with him. "Let go of me, I can walk!" We fell into step side by side as we meandered down the dirt road.

Billy stopped again and got out his binoculars. He squinted like it was hard to see. "There's some movement, but I can't tell what it is. It could be a deer or a dog." He started walking, so I did too. There was a crispness in the air, and the leaves were starting to turn. The grassy fields, the pine trees, even the dirt, it all smelled good. These were the kinds of smells you remember. Billy and I walked in silence. It was a good silence. The kind of silence when two good friends are just walking somewhere together.

"Get down!" Billy half whispered, half screamed. "Get low!" We ducked down on all fours. We sat there like frogs in the middle of the dirt road. "Billy, what's the matter now? Quit scaring me!"

"Shhhhh" He said again. We were still as statues. "What is it, Billy?"

"I'm still not sure. It looks bigger than a deer or a dog." We waited to see if anything else moved. Getting scared before we even got there made me want to turn around, but not Billy. "Let's keep walking. I've been out here before. Wait until you see how far we can run, Sally!" Then Billy took off running, leaving me standing there in the middle of the road. I took off after him. He wasn't going to leave me out here with who knows what lurking in the distance. Finally, we approached the gate to enter Hiram's Heaven.

"This is where we go in." The gate was unlocked, wide open. As soon as we got beyond it, branches started cracking, and the sound of hooves pounded out through the trees. Billy and I darted behind a big oak to see what was coming. A big herd of deer barreled towards us. They ran, jumped, and darted between the trees, and then they were gone. Right after that, two black dogs with big collars ran across the road. They didn't even notice us. We waited for the sounds to pass before we moved.

"What was that, Billy? Why do you think those dogs are chasing those poor deer?" I was concerned for the deer. "These are their fields. They were here first. Nature was here first, and they have beautiful eyes and big ears. There's no reason for those dogs to be chasing those deer." Billy seemed a little unsure about our situation. "Those might be hunting dogs, Sally. I didn't think of that." This required an explanation.

"I forgot it was deer hunting season." He stood there contemplating our next move.

"I didn't come out here to get shot, Billy. My mom will be very mad if you get us shot out here today." I always invoked Mom's name when I wanted something done.

"We're not going to get shot, Sally. I know exactly where we are, and you don't get shot out here." As we walked, I could hear the dogs barking in the distance.

The sun warmed my face. It felt good to be free like this. No one around, nowhere to go, nowhere to be. Just walking at our own pace with nothing but trees and air all around us. I wanted to twirl in the sunshine. I held out my arms and started to make big circles around Billy, like I was a bird flying around him. He did the same, and we weaved our way down the road in half circles around each other for the next few minutes. Nothing could hold us back. We were on our way to heaven.

The path came up, followed by a patch of thick pines and an opening to the fields. I knew right then; Billy had brought me to a special place. It went on as far as the eye could see. This must have been how the Indians felt when they gazed across their lands. A sense of openness and expanse that couldn't be captured in a word. It was a feeling of untouchable freedom.

"Are you ready to run?" Billy was grinning from ear to ear. This was the moment we had waited for. It was time to let go and run full force into the wind. You had to scream loud when you ran, and you had to run as fast as you can. That's the whole idea. You let go of everything and run blindly toward the horizon, wherever it may lead.

And with a war whoop, we were off! Screaming at the top of our lungs and running full speed through the tall grassy fields. This was heaven! We ran, and we ran, and we ran until we fell down. We rolled down a fluffy hill of grass that dropped toward a lake. Then we went back to the top and did it three more times. Finally, we lay on our backs, staring up at the sky. We watched clouds pass by and tried to name them. We guessed the time based on the position of the sun.

Right about then, we heard another ruckus coming from the woods. Gunfire rang out, and something ricocheted off a tree. I froze in the grass, too scared to sit up. Billy rolled over and sat up to peer over the grassy shield around us. More shots rang out, and he dove back down in a panic.

"Don't stand up, Sally! Stay low!" I did. I was terrified. The gunfire stopped. We waited. We could hear men's voices in the distance. "We better get out of here, Billy before we get killed! I want to go home right now." I stood up and brushed myself off, looking down at Billy still cowering in the grass. "I might be a kid, but I'm not stupid. I'm not going to sit out here and wait to get shot. Let's go." Billy wouldn't get up. He lay there face down in the grass, not moving. "Billy? Are you okay?" He didn't move. "Billy?" He was face down, his voice muffled by the grass.

"I rolled in something.".

"What do you mean you rolled in something?"

He turned over. Sure enough, he had cow dung all over him. Not just on his shirt or just on his pants, but all over him. He had rolled in a great big cow patty. He was covered. I put my hand over my nose and mouth as he rose from the grass. He smelled bad too. I took off running and could not stop laughing as I ran.

I've never felt so free as I did that day in Hiram's Heaven. Billy and I had the best of times. It was probably the closest to heaven I would ever get. And if I ever did get there again, I hoped Billy would be there too. He will always be my best friend.

Vicki Montet is an Emmy award-winning journalist and author of *The French Descendant*, her first Southern mystery novel. This tantalizing tale of true crime is tangled up in deep family secrets and the pursuit of a tell-all letter about a legendary assassination plot and the 1935 killing of Louisiana's most notorious politician, Huey Long. She's an avid traveler, photographer, and member of the Atlanta Writers Club. You can find her on LinkedIn and at VickiMontet.com.

Look for the rest of these stories and more as our contest winners and finalists grow their careers through the connections they make at the San Francisco Writers Conference.

Enter your work next time or join us at the next class or conference.

SFWriters.org

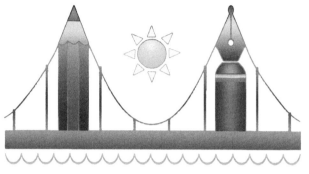

SAN FRANCISCO
WRITERS
CONFERENCE
Learn. Connect. Publish.

Made in the USA
Columbia, SC
03 December 2023

27115938R00075